I stared

upon the city of Komar, where it crouched upon high cliffs, girdled about with its mighty wall. Guardsmen in the colors of Prince Andar strode the watch about the circuit of that frowning battlement, and they bore torches in their hand to light their path.

By the light of those glimmering torches, I saw a strange and lovely thing. Fashioned all of gleaming metal, it floated upon the breeze as lightly as would a soap bubble. Slim and tapering it was, graceful as the Flying Carpet of Arabic legend, its prow curled back to shelter its riders.

This was the sky-sled we had carried off long ago from the Pylon of Sarchimus the Wise. The extinct Kaloodha had fashioned the flying thing a million years ago.

The moment my eyes fell upon it, I knew that I could delay no longer the satisfaction of that urge that gnawed with me, to search for my lost beloved, though all the wide world lay between us.

With Karn of the Red Dragon, to think was to act . . . I sprang over the parapet.

"Zorak snatched up his bow and loosed an arrow."

IN THE GREEN STAR'S GLOW

by
Lin Carter

Illustrated by
Michael Whelan

DAW BOOKS, INC.
DONALD A. WOLLHEIM, PUBLISHER

1301 Avenue of the Americas
New York, N. Y.   10019

The Green Star Saga

I.   UNDER THE GREEN STAR
                    (UY1185—$1.25)

II.   WHEN THE GREEN STAR CALLS
                    (UQ1062—95¢)

III.   BY THE LIGHT OF THE GREEN STAR
                    (UQ1120—95¢)

IV.   AS THE GREEN STAR RISES
                    (UY1156—$1.25)

V.   IN THE GREEN STAR'S GLOW
                    (UY1216—$1.25)

FIRST PRINTING, JANUARY 1976

1 2 3 4 5 6 7 8 9

DAW sf
BOOKS

PRINTED IN U.S.A.

For Kenorben, John, Susie, Jim, Wendy, and those of the Albanians who enjoy an old-fashioned yarn.

Contents

The Fourth Book:
KARN AMONG THE AMAZONS

The Fifth Book: SWORDS AGAINST PHAOLON

List of Illustrations

The First Book

LOST AMONG THE TREETOPS

1.

Many Partings

Joy held sway over the island kingdom of Komar, but over my heart there hovered a bitter cloud of black despair.

My friends and I, with the aid of Luck and Chance and the whim of Fate, had at last succeeded in breaking forever the iron grip of the Blue Barbarians upon the throne of Komar. The savage warrior horde, broken and decimated by a long and bloody night of invasion, battle, and siege, had fled by ship to sea and from there to shore. The scattered remnants of the once-mighty horde of Barbarians had slunk into the shadows of the sky-towering forest of gigantic trees like whipped curs. Never again would they menace the peace and security of the treetop kingdoms of the Green Star World.

Their day had passed, and a new day had dawned.

The gallant and courageous Prince Andar had been raised to the throne of his ancestors. Komar had its freedom, and a prince of the ancient blood to reign over that freedom. A day of celebration and festival had begun, such as the proud and age-old island realm had never known before.

In the bestowal of honors and the giving of gratitude, my friends and I were far from forgotten. Indeed, we stood foremost in the ranks of those who had helped to free the island city from its oppressors.

Zarqa the Kalood, Janchan of Phaolon, the Goddess Arjala, Parimus the science wizard, the immortal sage, Nimbalim of Yoth (aye, even sly, grinning, ugly Klygon, the thief who had become a hero), each of us in our turn were cheered and honored.

Nor was I, Karn, the savage jungle boy whose body held cupped within it the star-wandering spirit of an Earthling, overlooked in the bestowal of honors. Long and loud rang out the cheers when Prince Andar from the throne of his fathers called me forth to stand beneath the golden banner for the recital of my few poor deeds.

It should have been a happy day; for me it was a day of immeasurable gloom.

You who have followed thus far the journal of my exploits, adventures, and wanderings under the Green Star (if indeed any eye but my own will ever peruse this narrative of marvels) will understand the reason for the pall of sadness that froze my heart within me.

For there, at the very last, on the rooftop of the palace-citadel, with our arch-foe, Delgan of the Isles, at bay, my eyes, which had been blinded but now with sight renewed, gazed upon a sight of wondrous and pitiful enigma.

Niamh the Fair, Niamh my beloved, so long sought, so long lost, was restored to me at last, in a flashing instant of time. In the next breath she was torn from me again, and plunged into a desperate and unequal struggle against the very personification of doom.

The sky craft which the mad immortal, Ralidux, had stolen from the vault of treasures on the Isle of Ruins drifted low over the rooftop of the palace.

From the crest of the stone colossus wherein he had concealed himself, our dread enemy, Delgan, sprang into the craft and fought with my beloved princess for the controls.

Only Zorak, the loyal and stalwart bowman of Tharkoon, of us all had the presence of mind, in that terrible,

flashing instant, to ascend the stone limbs of the giant idol
and seize a fingertip hold on the tail of the floating craft
as it drifted idly away, borne on the winds of dawn.

We stood helpless, watching it float out of sight.

Zarqa and Parimus, in the air yacht of the science
wizard, had flown after the weightless craft, only to observe from a great distance as it floated from sight between the sky-tall trees of the mainland.

Their last glimpse had been one fraught with hideous
possibilities.

As it drifted from view between the prodigious boles of
the forest, *one* body had fallen from the craft to certain
death below.

But—*whose?*

Delgan, our azure-skinned arch-enemy, who had earned
his death a thousand times over for his treacheries and
betrayals?

Or Zorak, the strong and faithful bowman who had
come to the defense of Andar's realm?

Or—most horrible possibility of all—had it been the
frail and slender body of my beloved princess, overcome
by the grim strength of the traitor, Delgan?

Had he mastered her, and cruelly thrust her from the
cockpit of the craft, to hurtle down to a terrible death in
the black, worm-haunted abyss that was the floor of the
sky-tall forest of gigantic trees?

Search as they did, my friends returned to Komar with
that question unanswered, that mystery unsolved.

And that was the reason for the black cloud of despair
that hung over my heart on that joyous day of festival and
thanksgiving. . . .

The time had come for us to part, my friends and I.
Prince Parimus of Tharkoon, having assisted in the
conquest of the Blue Barbarians and the freeing of their
Komarian subjects, gathered his bowmen, bade us fare-

well, and entered his air yacht for the voyage back to his
own far realm.

With him as an honored guest went the thousand-year-
old sage and philosopher, Nimbalim of Yoth, whom Janchan and Zarqa had rescued from the slave pens of Calidar, the Flying City of the Black Immortals.

They had much in common, the science wizard and the
old philosopher. Together they would delve into the lost
sciences of the Kaloodha, the Winged Men, whose world-
old race was now extinct save for Zarqa alone.

After many farewells, they departed for Tharkoon.

They had lingered only to witness the marriage of Prince
Janchan of the Ptolnim and the Divine Arjala. It was Andar of the Komarians himself who wed these comrades of
mine, there on the steps below his throne, in the great hall
of his ancestral palace, ringed about by the lords and
nobles of his island realm.

There we watched, solemn and yet joyful, as Baryllus,
the High Priest of Karoga, god of Komar, celebrated the
holy nuptials. We stood smiling as Janchan clasped his
bride to his chest and sealed her lips with their first kiss.
Oh, it was a wondrous moment for all ... but wondrous
beyond beyond belief for Janchan of Phaolon and his
mate.

She had been a living goddess in Ardha; now she was
only a woman, and a bride.

I believe she had never been happier.

Then came the time of partings.

Prince Andar bade farewell to Parimus of Tharkoon
and his gallant bowmen, then turned to offer Janchan and
Arjala the hospitality of his palace for their honeymoon
(for strange as it seems, the custom familiar to us on
Earth is also known to the Laonese). As well, his hospitality was extended to Klygon, Zarqa, and myself, to remain in Komar as long as we wished, as his honored
guests. Weary and worn as we were from the perils and
privations through which we had all but recently passed,

his invitation was gratefully accepted. Indeed, there was little else that we could do, in all actuality, for in this strange and beautiful and terrible world of trees as tall as Everest, where the very cities of men cling to the upper branches like mere hornets'-nests, we had long since lost our bearings. Our ultimate goal was Phaolon the Jewel City, but no man in all of the Komarian kingdom, least of all ourselves, knew in which direction nor at what distance it lay.

So we made ourselves comfortable in Komar, for a time. My comrades were grateful for a chance to rest a while and enjoy the comforts of civilization, after the terrible trials of slavery, storm, shipwreck, and marooning we had undergone.

Not so, I.

Still the unknown fate of my beloved princess weighed upon my heart. Still the unanswered question of *which* of the three had fallen from the sky-ship echoed within my weary brain, repeating itself over and over.

Unable to sleep, despite the exertions of the day just past, I rose from my silken bed, donned my buskins, wrapped the scarlet loincloth about me, and belted on my glassy sword.

Restless, I went out upon the balcony of my tower room to gaze forth upon the night, thinking of Niamh.

The World of the Green Star has no moon to illuminate its skies by night, as does my native Earth. It revolves close to its sun of emerald flame, so close that, were it not for its eternal barrier of clouds which interpose themselves between the planet and its parent star, the burning heat of those green rays would scorch the last vestiges of life from the surface of the planet.

Alas, that same eternal and unbroken wall of clouds hide forever from view the innumerable stars of heaven, and the slender and elfin folk of this world—the Laonese, as they call themselves—are denied the splendors of the

star-strewn firmament. Hence the nights of Lao are black
as doom, in which no man may see his path.

I stared upon the city of Komar, where it crouched
upon high cliffs, girdled about with its mighty wall.
Guardsmen in the colors of Prince Andar strode the
watch about the circuit of that frowning battlement, and
they bore torches in their hand to light their path.

By the light of those glimmering torches, I saw a
strange and lovely thing. Fashioned all of gleaming metal
it was, but it floated upon the breeze as lightly as would a
soap bubble. Slim and tapering it was, graceful as the Flying Carpet of Arabic legend, its prow curled back to shelter its riders.

This was the sky-sled we had carried off long ago from
the Pylon of Sarchimus the Wise. The extinct Kaloodha
had fashioned the flying thing a million years ago.

The moment my eyes fell upon it, I knew that I could
delay no longer the satisfaction of the urge that gnawed
within me, to search for my lost beloved, though all the
wide world lay between us.

With Karn of the Red Dragon, to think was to act.
This trait had precipitated me into peril many times before now, and doubtless would do so again. A wiser man,
or a man less driven by his need, would have paused,
thought things out, consulted with his friends. But I
sprang over the parapet and clambered down the thick
vines as if they had been a ladder.

Lightly as a great cat, I dropped to the top of the cit-
adel wall. The guards had passed this way but a moment
before; still the light of their torches gleamed in the glistening gold metal of the sky-sled, where it drifted idly to
and fro on the breeze, tethered by its anchor-cable to a
stone bench.

It was the work of a moment to glide to where the
weird craft floated, to heave myself aboard. I lay flat in
one of the shallow depressions made for that purpose,
studying the controls. Often I had watched as Zarqa the

Kalood had flown the craft. The controls were few and admirably simple. There was no doubt in my mind that I could fly the craft.

Then, swiftly and unobtrusively, making certain that I was not observed, I returned to my quarters in the palace and took up my weapons and a warm cloak. In the great hall where the wedding-feast had recently concluded I selected provisions of meat and pastry, and a supply of the delicious if oddly colored foodstuff the Komarians prize, which resembles excellent cheese. There being no other beverage to hand, I scooped up as many bottles of the effervescent, gold-colored wine of the islands as remained unopened, and, returning to where my craft was moored, stored these provisions away in the tail-compartment, which was locked by a clever catch whose secrets I had learned from Zarqa.

Then, buckling myself in the safety harness, I detached and drew aboard the anchor-cable and stored it away in its place while the aerial vehicle floated out over the crooked streets and peaked roofs of Komar.

A moment later, my touch at the sensitive controls sent the silent and weightless craft winging its way out over the dark surface of the sea in the direction in which the sky craft had flown, bearing my beloved princess to a nameless and unknown doom.

Living or dead, I would find her, or perish myself in the attempt.

2.

Battle Amid the Clouds

As the sky craft which Ralidux had stolen from the treasure-vaults of the Ancient Ones drifted weightlessly across the roof of Prince Andar's besieged palace-citadel, Niamh—the Phaolonese princess whom I had come to love under the name of Shann of Kamadhong during my blindness, when we were castaways together on the desert isle of Narjix in the Komarian Sea—had no sooner freed herself from one attacker than a second thrust himself upon her.

The black superman from the Flying City, Ralidux, driven mad by his uncontrollable lust for Arjala the Living Goddess, had carried off Niamh from our desert isle under the mistaken assumption that she was none other than the superb young woman whom he desired above all else. Discovering his error, he had planned to hurl her slim body over the side of the flying vessel. But Niamh, tearing free of her bonds, and plucking from its secret sheath amid the tattered remnants of her garments, that slender, sacred knife which is, to every woman of the Laonese race, the final defense of her chastity, turned upon her kidnapper.

They fought together, there in the cockpit of the sky craft, as it drifted idly over the rooftops of Komar. At length my beloved princess succeeded in striking home: like the fang of a striking cobra, the slim bright blade sunk to its hilt in the heart of the Black Immortal and he toppled from the cockpit to fall to the rooftop far below.

Wrenching her blade from the heart of Ralidux in the instant of his fall, Niamh turned to seize control of the floating air vessel. But in the same moment of time a strange man with azure skin and subtle, crafty eyes sprang into the cockpit from the stony limbs of the colossal statue which loomed atop the palace roof.

Niamh stared at him dazedly. They had never so much as laid eyes on each other before, had Delgan of the Isles and the Princess of Phaolon, but this mattered little. The former Warlord of the Blue Barbarians had seized upon this trick of fortune to make his escape, and would permit no adolescent girl to deter him in his flight.

In one hand he bore that deadly crystal rod in which captive lightnings flickered—the *zoukar,* or death-flash—which Zarqa and Janchan and I had borne off long ago in our escape from the doomed and dying Pylon of the science magician, Sarchimus the Wise.

Leveling the powerful weapon at the wide-eyed girl—who crouched the length of the cockpit away, a slim, now gory, blade clenched in one small but capable fist—the traitorous Delgan was about to direct the furious ray of the crystal weapon against this unknown girl who stood in the way of his escape.

But then the bidding of caution made him stay his hand. The terrific power of the *zoukar* was a subject with which he was not completely familiar. To loose its frightful energies within the narrow confines of the cabin might be to damage the sky craft beyond all hopes of repair.

Therefore, with a swift motion, he thrust the crystal weapon into his girdle, and, with a tigerlike bound, flung himself upon the young girl who opposed him.

So swiftly did the mysterious blue man leap into the cabin—and so unexpectedly did he hurl himself upon her—that Niamh was taken by surprise. Suddenly, a hand like an iron vise clamped itself about her wrist, while the blue man flung his other arm about her waist, lifting her from the floor of the cabin. While she sought to plunge her slim blade into his heart, he strove to drag her to the edge of the cockpit and fling the hapless girl over the side.

In the fury of their combat, neither Niamh nor her assailant noticed Zorak the Bowman as he scaled the stony limbs of the colossus. He flung himself across space in an effort to reach the sky-ship before it floated away from the palace roof for a rescue attempt to succeed.

The outstretched fingers of the stalwart Tharkoonian brushed the tail-assembly of the flying craft . . . slipped, then clung. A moment later, the flying craft bore him away, out over the streets of the city. Then his dangling booted heels swung giddily above the tranquil immensity of the inland sea. And this was the last of the flying craft which I, Karn, saw as the Green Star rose up over the horizon to flood the world of the great trees with its emerald light.

Delgan had not dreamed that he would encounter any difficulty in overcoming the slight figure of the adolescent girl. For, although by no means as robust or as burly as were most of the Blue Barbarians, he was a full-grown man in his prime and possessed of a man's strength.

But the supple girl twisted lithely in his crushing grip, as agile as a writhing serpent. The girl fought furiously against the blue man as he struggled to thrust her over the side. Delgan soon discovered he had taken on a young wildcat.

She raked the sharp nails of one hand down the side of his face, slashing his cheek from eye-corner to chin. Blood spurted from his torn flesh; with a curse, he jerked his head back, fearing that with the next swipe of her vicious nails she might blind him.

Then a small but firm knee thudded into the pit of his stomach with staggering force. With a whoosh the air was driven out of his lungs as Niamh drove one sharp elbow into his ribs. Bent double, clutching at his belly, face streaming with blood, Delgan stumbled in retreat until he was backed against the control panel itself. Blinking open his eyes, which had been squeezed shut with pain, he saw the sunlight of the Green Star flash dazzlingly from the small, glittering blade of the girl's knife.

The gleam of the naked metal was no less deadly than the wrathful fires that burned fiercely in the girl's narrowed eyes.

Pampered child of the jewelbox cities though she was, Niamh of Phaolon fought like a tigress when she had to.

Facing her glittering blade, Delgan's bravery ebbed. Cunning and unscrupulous, it was ever his way to win with words or guile rather than to resort to physical action, which, in his warped view, was the way of the brute. The wily and devious Delgan had long ago discovered that he would trick and entangle those he sought to use in a web of words. So he tried it now, rather than trust his precious hide to the stinging kiss of that small, chaste blade.

"Would you slay me, then, witch-girl?" he panted. "I am no enemy of yours! Think: have ever we met, child? If not, then how could we be foes?"

"It was no friend who tried to thrust me over the side, stranger!" spat Niamh, the keen knife unswerving in her grip.

Delgan forced a bewildered laugh.

"But you have taken everything wrong, child! I sprang aboard this flying craft to aid you in piloting it to the palace roof, for I alone know the trick of the controls. And I leaped forward to steady you, for fear that the impact of my leap might toss you from your feet and over the side. Then, and, I'm afraid, without even giving me a moment to speak and to identify myself, you brought that wicked small knife into action. Even then, although attacked without warning, I was not provoked, but kindly thought to remove the weapon from you, lest in your hysteria you do yourself an injury. . . ."

The blue man's words were smoothly plausible, and the bewildered, almost hurt tones with which he uttered them came very close to disarming Niamh's suspicions. But the girl was no fool and remembered her own precise reactions, despite the sly-tongued villain's attempt to befuddle her.

"If you are my friend, first toss that curious crystal weapon over the side," she said keenly. Then, with a small, ironic smile, she added: "For, if we are friends, we need no weapons, now, do we?"

He nodded in a friendly fashion. "Certainly I will do so, to reassure you, mistress. But the crystal rod is no weapon; it is an instrument of the Ancients which sheds light in darkness. At any rate, I will surely do as you wish . . . but first, I think it not too much for me to ask of you a similar token in gesture of our friendship. Throw away that knife of yours, and I will do as you bid."

Niamh looked at him strangely.

"Do you not know that every woman of my race bears ever on her person the sacred knife that is called the 'Defender of Chastity'?" she murmured, puzzledly. "Or are you some savage outlander, unfamiliar with the code of civilization?"

Delgan, who was indeed just such a savage, albeit one who had rigorously schooled himself in the ways of the more civilized races of his world, bit his lip in silent fury at the slip. But not so much as a muscle twitched in his face to reveal his inward feelings.

"Of course, of course! I had forgotten!" he said, with an apologetic laugh. "Well, then, my girl, sheathe that holy knife of yours, or put it away . . . a naked blade is not drawn between comrades, you know!"

So cleverly devised was the verbal trap he had woven about her, that Niamh—although her every impulse screamed to retain the blade for instant use, if threatened—could not conjure up a good reason for not putting away the little knife. Keeping a wary eye on the smiling, seemingly friendly man, she reinserted the blade in its secret sheath, which was sewn in the lining of the garment wound about her breasts. When she had done so, she half expected the strange blue-skinned man to hurl himself upon her. But he did not.

"There we are, then; a truce between us?" he suggested genially.

"Perhaps," she said tentatively. "But you have not yet tossed overside the crystal rod you wear."

"This?" he said, smiling, drawing the death-flash from his girdle. "But it is too rare and precious to throw away, this artifact of the Ancients." Then the deadly crystal rod was pointed unswervingly at her heart.

"Do not move or reach for that wicked little knife of yours," he said softly. "But do exactly as I say. The deathly fires of lightning sleep in this rod, easy to awake, and it would be a pity to snuff out so young a life, to sear and shrivel so delectable a soft young body."

Niamh crimsoned and bit her lip at the mockery in his eyes, but she offered no resistance.

Then he reached for her.

3.

Over the Side

Delgan suddenly snatched back his hand with a shrill, unbelieving cry. For, out of nowhere, a green-feathered arrow had transfixed his hand. Paling to a muddy, unhealthy hue, his thin-lipped mouth pinched with pain, Delgan stared down at his right hand. The arrow had pierced completely through the bones of his wrist. Its gory-bladed point protruded from the other side of his arm. Red blood trickled down his hand to drip upon the cabin floor from numb fingertips.

In the next instant a deep, quiet voice spoke from somewhere behind Niamh:

"Do not give credence to his lying words, lady, for he is a faithless traitor, and the direst foe of your friends Janchan and Zarqa and Karn."

Niamh turned about to see the speaker of these words, and saw a tall, bronzed bowman in the forest-green and silver of Tharkoon. His powerful scarlet bow was at the ready, an arrow nocked in place to be loosed upon the instant, should the blue man try to fire the *zoukar* he still gripped in his uninjured hand.

While Delgan had sought to trap her in his wily web of words, the bronzed bowman had drawn himself up with a surge of his mighty arms until he straddled the tail-assembly of the sky craft. Then he had inched his way along the smooth, sleek fusilage of the streamlined flying vessel, until he crouched just behind the spacious cockpit. From that vantage point he had observed all which had transpired between the lissome girl and the smooth-tongued ex-Warlord of the Barbarian horde. His intervention had been a timely one. So intent had Delgan been upon the slim girl he sought to ensnare with his lies and half-truths and clever distortions of fact, his keen and watchful eyes fixed upon her elfin face, that he had not so much as glimpsed the burly bowman crouched atop the cowling. Had he so much as lifted his fixed gaze from Niamh's face for an instant, the encounter might have had a very different outcome.

Now holding his bow nocked and ready in one hand, the archer from Tharkoon swung his booted legs over the cowling and dropped like a great cat into the cockpit to stand protectively beside the bewildered Princess of Phaolon.

"He lies, lady, I swear it!" panted Delgan, his eyes wild, his calm controlled demeanor shaken for once. His mouth worked loosely and spittle foamed at the corners of his lips, to dribble down his chin. "He is a renegade—an outlaw!—who seeks to seize you and deliver you into the hands of your enemies. I, I alone, am your friend!"

His words were shrill and, for once, rang falsely on the ear. His very expression, wide-eyed, mouth working loosely, sweat beading his features, reeked of fear. Niamh did not believe him and shrank against the side of the towering bowman as the hysterical blue man gesticulated wildly, the death-flash forgotten in his hand.

The sky-ship borne on the swift wings of the morning breeze, had traveled a very great distance by this time. Indeed, the island city of Komar was by now lost from view somewhere behind them, cloaked from sight behind a pearly veil of morning mist. The Komarian Sea was not of any great breadth in these parts; indeed, the shoreline of the mainland was clearly in view dead ahead of their floating prow. They could see the immense boles of the

miles-tall trees soaring up out of the abyss of darkness
which was the floor of the world-encumbering forest.

The wind was carrying them directly into that mighty
rampart of mountain-high trees. The eyes of Zorak were
first to spot their peril, and with a grunt of surprise, let-
ting his red bow fall, the bowman stepped forward to
seize the controls and turn the prow aside before the hurtling craft drove into the mighty palisade of tree-trunks.

Eyes feral with desperation, goaded into viciousness
like a cornered rat, the blue man, with the arrow through
his wrist, fell into a defensive crouch as the bowman
stepped forward. Lips writhing back from his teeth, which
were bared in a fighting snarl, the blue man raised the
death-flash in one shaking hand.

"Back, you island dog, or I'll blast you where you
stand!" he whimpered.

"But, man, the trees!" grunted Zorak, pointing at the
wall of mighty trunks which swept up toward them. But
Delgan, where he crouched near the low edge of the cockpit had his back turned against that forward view, and
had no notion of the danger that was upon them.

"An old trick," he snarled with a shaky laugh, "to trap
a clever wolf. Do not move, on peril of your life, you
hulking brute—"

Zorak gestured helplessly as a great branch thrust into
their path, gold-foil leaves glittering in the light of the
Green Star. Then, ignoring the threat of the crystal rod,
the bowman turned and swept Niamh into his arms to
protect the girl from injury with his own brawny body
serving as her shield.

In the next instant the hurtling craft tore through the
mass of foliage. Leaves huge as a schooner's sails
whipped past them. The pointed nose of the flying ship
grated against rough bark and the fabric of the craft
shuddered under the rasping impact of the glancing blow.

Delgan staggered before the buffet as one great leaf
swept by him, knocking him from his feet. The backs of

his knees struck against the edge of the low cockpit with stunning force. With a screech of blood-chilling fear the blue man fell backward over the edge of the cockpit and disappeared from view, still clutching the *zoukar* in a deathlike grip.

An instant later, like a sleek projectile, the flying vessel whipped through the mesh of leaves and went wobbling drunkenly into open air again, still reeling from the glancing blow. Zorak threw himself to the edge of the cockpit and looked over. They were among the boles of the sky-tall forest by now, and only an abyss of impenetrable gloom was visible below. He could not even glimpse the dwindling mote of Delgan's writhing form as the unfortunate Warlord fell to his unquestioned death half a mile below, where great pallid worms squirmed through the fetid darkness of the forest's floor. . . .

And *this* was the terrible sight which Zarqa and Prince Parimus glimpsed from afar as they pursued the flying ship in the air yacht of the science wizard: one minute body falling from the craft as it slipped between the soaring tree-trunks and vanished from their view.

From that great distance, of course, they could not tell which of the three riders had fallen to his or her death in the black abyss beneath the lurching keel. . . .

The sky craft slid between two towering boles and drifted into an uncanny world of more-than-earthly beauty.

Only those who have visited the World of The Green Star can picture the incredible vista that met the eyes of Zorak and Niamh. In every direction trees of dark scarlet wood towered, their trunks thicker than the mightiest of skyscrapers, soaring aloft mile upon mile to thrust their vastness of golden foliage into the stratosphere. Between these lofty boles, great shafts of pellucid jade-green sunlight fell, shining through momentary rents in the eternal cloud-veil whose silver mists shielded the planet from the fierce emerald fires of its parent star. Here and there between the towering trees floated dragonflies as huge as Percherons, drifting on wings like sheeted opal. There, stretched on mile-long cables between the mighty branches, a spider web of colossal dimensions hung, its sticky strands thick enough and strong enough to hold rampaging mammoths captive. Clinging by sucker-disks to the underside of branches whose breadth was that of six-lane highways, golden and green and crimson lizards, fearsome and enormous as fabled dragons, clung.

It was an awesome and mysterious scene of strange and terrible beauty, such as my native Earth can nowhere display. But to Niamh the Fair it was known and familiar, for the gem-bright city of her birth nestled somewhere in aboreal giants such as these, and these incredible vistas were all that she had ever known.

But to Zorak the Bowman it was a weird new world of unknown marvels, for home to the brawny archer was the city of Tharkoon on its isolated peninsula thrusting out into the calm waves of the Komarian Sea, and the giant trees of Lao were an unexplored mystery to him. Thus he gaped with amazement upon the sights that lay everywhere.

The winds that had propelled the sleek and weightless projectile across the narrow straits of sea between the isle of Komar and the mainland had died now. No matter how strong the morning breeze might blow, it broke and died against the looming rampart of the arboreal titans. Thus the sky craft floated more slowly now, drifted idly to and fro, eventually coming to rest between the two segments of a forked twig as large as a siege catapult. Waking from his entranced fascination, the bowman bent in puzzlement over the controls, eventually finding the switch that killed the power-source which drove the engines of the flying ship.

"Well, where to now, my lady?" he asked, once the danger of collision with one of the huge branches was past. "Delgan will trouble us no more, but we must be making our return to Komar, where your friends wait."

Niamh turned to him eagerly. "Is it true, brave bowman, what I glimpsed in that brief moment above the palace roof? Has the boy, Karn, recovered his vision? Is it true that his eyes are healed?"

The Tharkoonian nodded. "Aye, lady, but whether it was from the cures slow nature works in her own good time, or from the science magic of my master, Parimus the Wise, who treated the youth's eyes, I do not know. But Karn can truly see again."

"I thank all Gods," she breathed, tears glittering on her thick lashes. "And Prince Janchan, and the Goddess Arjala, and somber, unspeaking Zarqa the Kalood, my friends who rescued me from the Flying City . . . they too live and are well and unhurt?"

"Aye." He nodded again. "All have come safely through our recent adventures in battle against the Blue Barbarians who held the island city of Komar and exiled her gallant heir, Andar."

"Then let us be about and back to this city of Komar of which you speak, so that we may rejoin our comrades," bade the girl breathlessly.

But when the bowman, obedient to her wishes, bent to the controls again nothing he could do could rouse the dormant engines into life. Some secret switch, it seemed, must first be engaged; but which it was, he did not know.

Weightless as a log upon the bosom of a stream, and as dead and lifeless, the sky craft hung moored between two branches . . . and they were lost, marooned half a mile above the world, in a part of the giant forest which even Niamh the Fair, for all her travels, had never visited before.

But not alone.

A deep-throated, menacing hiss woke Niamh from her frowning reverie as she bent over the panel, studying the multitude of dials, striving to remember which knobs and switches Ralidux had touched to pilot the craft.

She looked up into a snarling visage straight from the netherpits of some jungle hell ... looked into the naked fangs and yawning jaws and lambent yellow gaze of a monster lizard, which had slithered out upon the nearer of the twin branches until it crouched now with twitching tail only an arm's reach from the open cockpit.

4.

Dragon's Blood

One single glance at the crouching monster, and Niamh knew it for a dreaded *ythid,* the scarlet dragon of the treetops. Twice as long as a full-grown Bengal tiger, and many times its equal in sheer ferocity, the *ythid* was the most formidable of opponents.

And Zorak had only his bow!

Without a moment wasted on hesitation, the mighty archer from Tharkoon snatched up his bow and quiver. An instant later he had nocked and loosed an arrow into the snarling face of the tree-dragon. The hissing shaft glanced off the dragon's scarlet mail, however, without causing it hurt.

Zorak's second arrow caught the brute more effectively. The barbed shaft flew between the yawning jaws of the monster lizard and sank into the roof of its mouth.

Uttering a shrill screech like a steamboat's whistle, the dragon writhed about, snapping and champing its jaws in a vain effort to hurt the unseen adversary whose sting sent red pain lancing through its minuscule brain. The feathered shaft shattered into fragments at one snap of those powerful jaws.

Zorak steadied himself on the edge of the cockpit, and directed his third shaft at the most vulnerable spot on the entire body of the *ythid*: its burning eye.

But nature has armed the scarlet tree-dragons of the

33

World of the Green Star with a tough and horny integument where it is not otherwise mailed in a heavy layer of
serpent-scales. This integument extends even to the eyes
of the *ythid;* for the transparent membrane that can be
lowered to protect the dragon's vision is thick and durable
as a leather shield. Useless, Zorak's shaft went glancing
away into the great golden leaves which fluttered in the
breeze from the end of this branch.

An then the dragon pounced.

Niamh shrank back against the bucket-seats of the flying ship, fingers pressed against lips pale with fear.

The sucker-armed foreclaws of the dragon closed crush-
ingly about Zorak's upper arm, dragged him from his
place in the cockpit, and drew him into the reach of those
terrible jaws.

His right arm immobilized by the grip of the *ythid,*
Zorak was unable to direct another shaft at his pain-mad-
dened adversary. He let the bow fall from his hand, and
twisted about so that his booted feet struck the snarling
dragon in the mouth. Angrily hissing, the monster lizard
snapped at the booted feet which clouted it full in the
snout. Daggerlike fangs clicked together on the loose,
folded-back tops of the bowman's boots. Despite the
toughness of the seasoned leather, it was ripped to shreds
between the gashing fangs.

In a moment, Zorak himself would meet the same fate,
Niamh knew.

The princess had known a pampered and luxurious life
in her jeweled city. Danger, or hardship, or even discomfort, had seldom been permitted to roil or trouble the
calm serenity of her cushioned existence. But the perilous
adventures which had befallen the Princess of Phaolon in
the last few months had tested the fiber of her spirit. The
girl had found strength and courage and keen, wary,
quick-witted resources within her, whose very presence
she could never otherwise have expected.

Now, when her stalwart companion stood in imminent

peril of destruction, it was not the way of Niamh to cower, trembling in dread. Instead the brave girl snatched up the only weapon to hand—her small blade. With this clenched in one firm little fist, she sprang forward lithely over the sleek nose of the craft, and leaped upon the dragon's back.

Busily engaged in striving to mangle Zorak's legs into a red pulp, it is doubtful if the *ythid* was even aware of Niamh's slight weight as the girl sprang upon its back. It continued snapping and striking at Zorak's kicking feet, while the bowman, still held in that crushing grip, fought and struggled to keep free of the dragon's jaws. For if once those jaws closed upon his limb, the stalwart bowman would be maimed and crippled for life.

Niamh clambered up the slope of the *ythid*'s back and neck until she could reach its most vulnerable point with the small knife she held.

She drove the knife into the monster's left eye.

But her blade was small and the horny membrane protecting the orb of vision was tough and slick, and the knife dealt the dragon only a slight wound, a mere scratch.

However, the *ythid* felt the slim knife go scraping down its outer eye and jerked back instinctively. In order to hold itself in this recoiled position, it was forced to relinquish its grip on the bowman. The viselike grip of the dragon's hooked claws loosened and Zorak fell back against the sleek metal prow of the air ship.

His shredded boots swung out over the edge of the abyss as he slid down the curved, glistening fusilage of the ship. In desperation, Zorak flung out one strong hand and seized the top edge of the crystal windshield, halting his plunge over the edge.

Below his dangling legs the world fell away into a dim abyss miles deep. The nearest branch below him was some two hundred feet farther down, where immense and gauzy waxen blossoms swayed in the wind. Peering down, the bowman felt beads of cold sweat break out on his brow. Better by far the quick, mercifully brief death between the dragon's jaws, than the long endless nightmare of that miles-long fall to the gloom-thick bottom of the world. . . .

As the dragon reared and swerved its cruel jaws about to snap at the thing on its back, whose slight weight it now noticed, the sudden shift of its stance dislodged Niamh from her precarious perch between its shoulders.

She slid down the dragon's back until her slide was halted by encountering the dorsal fins that ran in a sawtoothed row down the monster's body to the tip of its lashing tail.

The *ythid* craned its head about, snapping viciously at the intrepid girl who dared ride it like a tame steed. Against those formidable fangs, Niamh's little knife was a flimsy toy. The girl gasped, and shrank back from the lunge of that snarling snout.

Zorak, dragging himself back to a more secure footing, caught up his bow and quiver again from where they had fallen. With the unconscious ease born of long practice, he fitted an arrow to the bowstring and drew it taut in less time than it takes to describe the action.

The dragon's head was turned away, so he aimed the barbed shaft at the comparatively soft throat of the *ythid*, directly beneath the hinge of its jaws, where the scales grew small and few.

The arrow hissed through space, and sank halfway to the feather in the lizard's unprotected throat.

Voicing a strangled squawk, the *ythid* reared up, flailing out with both hooked forepaws, gasping for air. Blood gushed from its straining jaws; blood flowed in a scarlet river down its throat to choke off its breath.

"*Jump clear!*" Zorak boomed.

Niamh released her hold on the dragon's bladed spine and half leaped, half fell to the rough surface of the branch. And not a moment too soon!

Death numbed the small brain of the tree-reptile even

in the moment that it reared erect. Its sucker-like feet lost their grip. It sagged ... crumpled ... struck its head against the edge of the branch, and fell over.

It was gone.

Where Niamh crouched, breathless, her heart pounding violently, the curvature of the branch rounded steeply. Only the rough indentations of the bark surface afforded her a handhold and foothold. Now that the worst was over, the girl sagged wearily, as nervous reaction drained the strength which desperation had lent her slim body.

It was Zorak who saw with a thrill of alarm that she was pale to the lips and close to swooning. Even as he looked he saw her hands go limp, relaxing their hold.

He sprang from the prow of the flying craft, throwing himself across empty space, to seize hold of the nearer of the great gold-foil leaves.

Then he dropped down to where Niamh sprawled near a puddle of dragon-gore. With one strong hand he caught her arm and half-dragged her higher up on the top of the limb, where her footing would be more secure.

Gasping, as realization of her peril suddenly flooded through her, the princess clutched the rough edges of the bark and held on for dear life.

But Zorak's leap had dangerously off-balanced him, and he held only the edge of a thin leaf. True, the leaf was as enormous as a ship's sail, but still it was tissue-thin.

And it tore.

As fate would have it, his feet, kicking out for a purchase on the branch, skidded and slipped in the fresh-spilled blood his own barbed shaft had torn from the dragon's throat.

He slipped, lost his balance, and fell.

Niamh uttered a choked cry and closed her eyes, willing the terrible moment not to have happened. But it had, and the brave and gallant Zorak of Tharkoon had fallen from the branch of the great tree to a horrible death far, far below.

The young girl was alone, helpless, lost; lacking the strong arm, the fighting courage, and the comforting companionship of a comrade in peril.

She crept to the edge of the branch and peered over, to see if the falling body of the bold, courageous archer had already dwindled into the depths below.

5.

The Opal Tower

Below the mighty branch by whose edge the Princess of Phaolon crouched, the world fell away into the unbroken gloom of the abyss far, far below. Branch upon branch thrust from the huge tree to which she clung, their thickening veils of golden leaves obscuring her vision. Thus, Niamh could see nothing of the fate which had befallen the gallant bowman, although she feared the worst.

Alone now, and disconsolate, the girl wandered back to where the powerless sky craft was securely wedged in the fork of the twiglet. Although she strove to reenergize the mystery engines which drove the flying ship, its secret eluded her as it had eluded Zorak the Bowman. Eventually, she gave up the attempt.

By this point the day had progressed toward the noon hour, and the Green Star stood at the zenith of the mist-shrouded sky. Niamh became aware of a growing hunger, and realized that she had eaten nothing in more hours than she could number. She searched the cabin of the sky-ship, but if any supplies of liquids or food had been stored aboard the craft by Ralidux, she could not find them.

Niamh was a child of this strange and savage world and knew that survival among the enormous trees was a continuous struggle. One could only mourn a fallen comrade for so long. Soon the practical matters of finding food

and drink and a haven for the night which would afford
some safety from prowling predators must take precedence
over one's sorrow.

She replaced her slim knife in its hidden sheath. Then
she took up the great bow of Zorak and the quiver of arrows that had fallen from his hand when he had sprung to
her assistance. Armed with these, the resourceful princess
set about procuring a meal for herself.

Climbing to the upper rondure of the branch to which
the ship was moored, she followed the curving bough for a
time, her keen eyes searching the leaves for game. Soon
she came upon a fallen leaf the size of a canoe. Drying, it
had curled into a long, slender, trough-shaped container,
and she was relieved and heartened to find the leaf damp
with a quantity of morning dew. Shaded from the rays of
the Green Star by the vast branch directly above, the
dewdrops within the curled leaf had not as yet evapo-
rated. Therefore she stooped, cupped her hands, and
drank her fill.

It may seem strange to my reader that a full-grown girl
could quench her thirst on a few drops of dew (if any
Earthling's eye but my own shall ever peruse these journals in which I have recorded the narrative of my adventures on this distant world), but such was indeed possible
on this planet of endless marvels. For here, where trees
grow taller than Everests, dragonflies grow to the size of
horses, and spiders are dangerous and man-killing predators, dewdrops are so huge as to each contain a pailful of
water.

I have never been able to figure out the weird, dispro-
portionate sizes on the World of the Green Star. On that
planet, either humans alone retain their terrestrial size,
while every other thing has grown tremendously larger, or
all other forms of life but the human are of natural size,
while men and women are minuscule. The immense size
of dewdrops may indeed be a clue pointing to the latter
theory, for on Earth, the surface tension which holds a

drop of water together is too feeble to sustain a waterdrop to any particular size. Therefore, unless the laws of nature are radically different on the Green Star World, the evidence suggests that people are very small.

I have no idea if this chain of reasoning is correct or false. The mysteries of Lao are innumerable, and during my days on this strange planet I have penetrated to the core of very few of them.

At any rate, having satisfied her thirst, and after laving her face and hands in the cool, pure fluid, Niamh rose refreshed and conscious now of an overpowering hunger.

She continued on down the branch, striding toward the place where it joined at last to the mighty trunk of the tree. Born and bred to their life in the arboreal heights, the Laonese are as surefooted as cats and utterly fearless of heights, as well as racially immune to vertigo; had it not been so, the race would have died out long ago. Therefore, Niamh traversed the length of the branch with careless ease, treading a narrow and perilous rondure which would doubtless have unmanned the most intrepid of Terrene Alpinists, at a height unthinkable.

And at the end of the branch she found a mystery.

There, where the branch joined with the soaring trunk of the giant tree, a tower rose. It was unlike any building which Niamh had ever seen before.

For one thing, it was fashioned of some smooth, glassy substance like a ceramic, and it seemed as tough and durable as porcelain. The coloring of the peculiar stone was that of an opal, filled with bewildering and changeful hues: peacock blue, iridescent bronze, fiery crimson, gold. It seemed to be built all in one piece, like some enormous piece of cast metal, or a structure of organic crystal somehow grown to a preconceived design.

Stranger even than these marvels was the manner in which it was built. It was a slim, tapering spire whose gliding curves and sleek lines bore little or no resemblance to any style of architecture with which Princess of Phaolon was familiar. It was weirdly alien.

Now, Niamh had never beheld the Pylon of Sarchimus the Wise, in which Prince Janchan, Zarqa the Kalood, and I, had been imprisoned during our stay in the Dead City of Sotaspra.* The Dead City had been composed of spires and domes similar to this Opal Tower in composition and design. Sotaspra had been the handiwork of Zarqa's own people, the Kaloodha, a long-extinct race of Winged Men who had flourished a million years before.

The Princess of Phaolon did not guess that the Opal Tower was a survival from that lost age. Nonetheless she was curious. She approached the base of the spire with trepidation, being careful that she should not be seen—for there was no way of telling whether or not the Opal Tower was occupied, and if so, by what.

As she drew nearer to the enigma, she saw certain curious details that she had not noticed before. For instance, the spire seemed to have no windows, although there was something about halfway up the soaring wall that resembled a balcony. For another, the way the opalescent colors swirled and crawled with every change of the light lent the weird minaret the illusion of being *alive*.

The girl felt the pressure of unseen eyes upon her, and this sensation of being watched grew stronger the closer she approached to the glimmering spire. But she ignored this feeling consigning it to mere imagination.

At the base of the building, a tall, slender opening appeared. It was a doorway or portal of some kind, although in shape and proportion and design it resembled no such entryway that Niamh had ever seen.

The door—if it *was* a door—was open.

Niamh crouched behind a huge golden leaf, chewing her bottom lip in an agony of indecision. The tower afforded her shelter and protection against the night, which

---

* As described in the second volume of these memoirs which I edited under the title of *When the Green Star Calls*. —*Editor*.

would be upon her in a few more hours. And it did not *seem* to be occupied; at least, there was no sign or token of present occupancy which met the eye. The tower had obviously been abandoned by its mysterious builder long ago, and might have stood thus, untenanted, for ages.

The girl hefted the bow of Zorak, which she carried nocked and ready. Even if the tower was inhabited, the tenant might not be unfriendly; and even if he was, it was not as if she were unarmed or unable to defend herself.

Determinedly setting her small jaw, Niamh the Fair rose lithely to her feet and strode toward the tall, pointed doorlike opening, the bow of Zorak held at the ready, her flowerlike face set in a resolute expression.

She entered by the tall opening without hesitation ... and vanished.

Then followed a most peculiar and frightening thing: The doorway closed, like a *mouth*.

Where, but a moment before, there had been a peaked, pointed gap, the wall of the Opal Tower now presented a smooth, unbroken surface: a surface, moreover, whose changeful colors, suddenly, flushed crimson.

Crimson as human blood. . . .

The Second Book

SLAVES OF THE SCARLET HORDE

6.

The Warrior Women

After a few moments I learned how to control the sky-sled and sent the diminutive craft speeding in a direction which, on my home world, we would have called north.

Directions on the World of the Green Star are particularly difficult to ascertain to a nicety. The Laonese seem never to have invented the compass, either because they have little need for such an instrument, or because ferrous metals such as iron and steel are exceptionally rare upon their planet. On the world of my birth, it is not difficult to discern the cardinal directions, at least, from mere observance of the sun's position in the heavens. On the planet of the great trees, however, this is seldom possible, due to the immense cloud-barrier which shields the surface of Lao from the fierce emerald beams of its primary. The silvery layer of impenetrable mists serve to scatter and diffuse the rays of the Green Star, spreading her luminance across the veiled heavens.

Komar soon dwindled behind me and was lost in the immensity of the dark sea. The islands of the archipelago floated by beneath the keel of my craft. Before long the shores of the mainland hove on the gloomy horizon, one colossal wall of monstrous trees whose mighty boles lifted up their leafy crest miles above the surface of the planet.

Slowing the velocity of the sky-sled, I drifted between the soaring tree-trunks and entered the gloom of the world-forest. Somewhere along this coast the aerial vehicle bearing Delgan and Zorak and Niamh the Fair had vanished from the knowledge of men. But where?

Their vessel could have entered the sky-tall woods at any point along the coast for scores or hundreds of miles in either direction. For a moment the immensity of my task overwhelmed me and the heart of Karn the Hunter sank within his breast. How, in all this vast, uncharted wilderness, to find the elusive mote that was the sky vessel? To seek the proverbial needle in the haystack seemed considerably simpler. . . .

After a while, my spirits rose within me. Difficult, even impossible, my task might consume months or perhaps years. But I was determined to undertake the search, whether it prove fruitless or not. To hunt, to search, to seek—whether or not with success—was preferable to doing nothing. Far rather would I roam the worldwide forests of this strange world forever, than to search not at all.

It was not long before I was forced to a realization that I must wait for dawn before attempting to begin my search for Niamh the Fair. Darkness amid the giant trees was absolute and unbroken, and the sled bore no running-lights. In this dense gloom I might float past the vessel of my beloved princess without knowing it. Moreover, it was dangerous to go blundering about in the blackness like this.

Therefore I slowed the forward velocity of the sky-sled to a mere crawl and watched for a safe place to berth the vehicle for the night. Before long I felt huge leaves brush the underside of the sled and discovered a twig which thrust up from the side of one great branch. I call it a "twig" for that is what it was; nonetheless, it was as wide about and of such a length as to have made a schooner's mainmast back on Earth.

Unlimbering my mooring grapnel, I soon secured the

sled to the twig and settled down for slumber. The confines of the sled were adequate for this purpose, and the nights on the Green Star planet were almost tropic in their warmth. But I could not find the rest I sought, nor did sleep come easily to one so troubled in his thoughts as I was. Fears for the safety of Niamh disturbed my mind, and unease for the future made me restless.

After tossing and turning for what seemed like hours, I managed to fall into a doze from which only the green-gold radiance of dawn awoke me . . . that, and the spear-point whose cold blade touched the smooth flesh just above my heart . . . .

My captors were, as it turned out, captresses. A band of young girls had crept upon me in the dim morning, and had clambered out upon the twig to which I had tethered my weightless craft. They were a wild-looking lot, with tangled hair and sunburned faces, clad in brief garments made of tanned leather hides which barely served to cover their lissome bodies and long naked legs. Sharp daggers were sheathed at their waist or strapped by thongs of gut to slim brown thighs. Many carried spears fashioned from long thorns, while others carried bows and arrows. There were an even dozen of them, and most were my age—that is, the teen-aged body my spirit wore.

Some looked as young as ten or eleven, but most of the wild girls were around fourteen.

Despite their tender years and their sex, I could not help noticing that they handled their weapons with the careless ease that comes to those who are long accustomed to using them.

I lay quietly, not moving, saying nothing, while they looked me over scornfully and chattered among themselves. Then one prodded me with her spear.

"You, boy! How did you come to be here in this flying thing? And from where? Speak, or I'll plunge my blade into your scrawny chest!"

The girl who addressed me so scornfully was a long

legged hoyden of perhaps thirteen, her supple form clad in a scrap of hide which bared one pink-tipped breast.

"I am Karn," I replied quietly. "I am searching for lost friends who are somewhere hereabouts in a flying vessel much like this one. We are from Komar—"

"Komar?" the young girl repeated with a sniff. "I never heard of it, nor is it anywhere about."

"Nevertheless, it was from Komar that I voyaged last evening," I said.

She looked me over narrowly, fierce disapproval written on her snub-nosed, freckled face. Despite her warlike aspect and savage raiment, she was very beautiful in the way that young girls are beautiful; that is, in the burgeoning promise of the womanhood to come.

Like most of the dwellers in the treetop cities, she had ivory skin, drifting thistledown hair of silvery gold, and eyes as green as emeralds, set amid thick sooty lashes. Her lithe and supple body was slim as a young panther, without so much as an ounce of superfluous flesh. She was intensely exciting.

While pondering my fate, or my story, or perhaps both, the train of her thought was interrupted by the query put to her by another of the band, like herself, somewhat older than the little girls.

"What shall we do with him, Varda? Slay him? He is a *man* after all, and fit only for the knife."

The girl who said this had flesh like old parchment and brilliant huge eyes that glared wrathfully at me through the floating locks of her silken hair. She looked to be fifteen, and her breasts were covered.

One of the littler girls, who was about ten and wore nothing at all except for a strip of hide wound about her loins, leather sandals on her feet, and the strap supporting her quiver of arrows across her boy-smooth breast, giggled.

"Let's keep him for a slave, Varda," she urged with a malicious grin at me.

I felt distinctly uncomfortable.

"No," returned the older girl who had spoken before, and whose name I later learned to be Iona, "let us slay him now. He will grow into a man, otherwise, and do with us as the others of his vile kind would have done. Therefore, he deserves to die. I vote—*death!* Death to the man-cub!"

"Death!" hissed the naked ten-year-old, an expression of most unchildlike vindictiveness on her pretty face. I began to sweat, and to calculate my chances of wresting the thorn-spear from the strong hands of Varda before she could drive it through my heart.

As it turned out, I had little to fear. Some sort of rivalry existed between the two older girls, Varda, the nominal leader of this band of teen-aged Amazons, and Iona. Whatever Iona urged, Varda automatically opposed. And, I imagine, vice versa. So the bare-breasted Varda obstinately refused to turn me over to the eager blades of the other little savages, and ordered me securely trussed and borne along.

The girl Amazons, apparently, had been camping out overnight on a hunting expedition, and were en route to their hideout when the luminance of dawn had caught and flashed in the mirror-bright metal of the sky-sled, attracting their attention and curiosity.

They dragged me from the craft with my wrists stoutly bound behind my back. This was done with many a slap and kick and scratch of sharp nails. All of this I endured in silence, as I also endured the more intimate insults they subjected me to. For they stripped me bare and mocked me for my scrawniness and laughed at my nakedness and humiliation. I ignored this treatment as best I could, and maintained an impassive mien.

Off down the bough they led me, laughing when I tripped and fell, flogging me to my feet again with a switch laid against my rear. At length, wearying of mocking and striking one who neither complained nor winced nor cried out, they simply drove me along with thumps of their spear-butts. The younger girls, scampering along like wild naked little forest nymphs, giggled mischievously and made loud comments on my nude boyhood, but the older girls ignored me after a time.

We descended by a length of rope to a lower branch, and while the girl warriors clambered down as lithely as so many small monkeys, I was lowered like a bale of goods at the end of a line, much to the merriment of the girl-children. Then we followed the second branch until it intersected with another, and so on until by noon, when we reached the camp of the girl savages, I was thoroughly and hopelessly lost. I could not then understand why they had left behind my aerial craft, my weapons, which were superior to their own rude arms, and my stores and provisions. Later I came to the conclusion that their hatred and loathing of all things male was so excessive and virulent that it extended even to those things made by the hands of men.

In conceiving of this notion, incidentally, I was later proved wrong, as shall be seen.

So it was that I became the male captive, the only captive, of a wild band of prepubescent savages.

It was an experience which I would not wish on even the most dire and deadly of my enemies.

7.

An Unexpected Ally

Zorak the Bowman awoke groggily from the impact of his fall, and for a time could scarcely believe his good fortune in being still alive.

He found himself in the embrace of a monstrous flower whose thick red petals had cushioned and gently broken his fall from the branch above. Had he landed on the bare branch, or upon any other possible surface, he would surely be dead by now, or at least seriously injured. For he had fallen nearly three hundred feet. Only the soft, yielding petals of the giant flower, which were surprisingly strong and elastic, had saved him from almost certain death.

He lay there woozily for a time in the velvety embrace of the vast blossom, swinging to and fro in the breeze, before attempting to rise. When he did make the attempt, he found it impossible to do so, for the flower was of a peculiar nature in that it fed itself by trapping and absorbing the enormous insects who flew between the gigantic trees. The upper surface of its velvety petals was lined with slender, tough scarlet tendrils which snapped tightly about any object or organism which blundered into them. The unwary insect who settled on the tempting blossom, hoping to drain its sweetness, soon found itself hopelessly enmeshed in the thin tendrils.

Zorak struggled against the embrace of the blossom for

"Zorak struggled against the embrace of the blossom."

a time, but it was no use. Strength alone, even the iron
strength of his magnificent and athletic body, would not
suffice to free him of the tenacious grasp of the tendrils.
They clung lightly but firmly about his limbs and torso, in
such a manner that he could not apply leverage. Had he
been able to do so, he might well have torn free with a
surge of his mighty muscles. But every inch of him was
clasped in the coils of the scarlet tendrils, and he was
helpless.

He was doomed to suffer a slow and agonizing death.

After a time, Zorak discovered that the blossom held
another captive besides himself. It was an immense insect,
whose scarlet chitin-clad body and antennae-pronged
head and multiple limbs closely resembled an Earthly ant.

Such creatures are known to the Laonese as *kraan*, and
were known to be coldly logical of mind, utterly emotionless, and of an almost human intelligence. They were also
feared as deadly and implacable enemies of all other
races, in particular the race of men. All too well do I
remember the terror the albino troglodytes felt for them,
during the time when Klygon and I were held captive in
the subterranean warrens of the cave-primitives.

Zorak could tell that the giant red ant was aware of his
presence, but did not think of addressing his companion
in misfortune, any more than you or I would think of attempting to strike up a conversation with a beast. It came
as quite a shock to him when the captive *kraan* addressed
him in a buzzing, toneless, clicking equivalent of human
speech.

"It serves no purpose to struggle against the grip of the
flower, manling. Wiser to rest and conserve your strength,
and wait for the fall of darkness," said the monster insect.

Zorak jerked his head around in amazement. The
mteallic sounds while resembling speech, could only have
come from the tongueless killer-ant. After a moment of
dazed surprise, he spoke in return.

"Am I losing my wits, *kraan,* or did you speak just now?" he demanded.

The insect jerked its brow antennae toward him in a gesture very much like a human nodding aquiescense.

"Xikchaka spoke."

Zorak muttered a dazed oath. "Never before have I heard that the mighty *kraan* of the restless hordes could converse with the tongue of men," he observed.

"Nevertheless, it is so, remarked the *kraan,* whose name seemed to be Xikchaka. "Among ourselves, we of the hordes have another means of conveying intelligence. But from those of your kind, manling, whom we have enslaved, we have gradually come to understand and to duplicate your mode of speech."

This time, Zorak had listened closely and had also watched the mouth of the great ant. Its head was a featureless casque, a helmet of smooth, slick, horny chitin. Its eyes were like complex black jewels carved in many facets. The light of intelligence shone in those cold eyes, for all that the voice it uttered was devoid of inflection and the fact itself was incapable of any change of expression.

The mouth of the *kraan* was merely an opening in the underside of its tapering helmet of a head. Bladelike members sprouted in it, and at either corner of the orifice small mandibles branched, like the claws of a lobster. In reproducing the phonemes of human speech, the *kraan* cleverly manipulated these implements in a very complex manner. The harsher consonants were made by grating, clashing, or scraping the mandibles against the bladelike cutting surfaces within the orifice itself. The softer consonants and the vowels were accomplished by rasping the backside of the toothed claws against the smooth chitin of the creature's muzzle. The soft plosives and the more breathy vowels were beyond the capabilities of the *kraan* to duplicate. This left gaps in its speech which took a little getting used to before you could clearly understand its words. The more they conversed, the easier it became for the Tharkoonian archer to comprehend the words of its weird and inhuman companion in peril.

After they had talked for a time, Zorak renewed his struggles against the many small, glossy tendrils with which the inner surfaces of the crimson petals were coated so furrily. Again, as before, his struggles resulted in failure. And again Xikchaka the giant ant cautioned him to conserve his strength and await the coming of night, or, as the *kraan* phrased it, the "dark-time."

"Why?" Zorak asked peevishly. "What happens when night falls?"

"The flower petals close," advised the insect-creature.

"I fail to see how that will benefit us," said the bowman.

"As the petals begin to close, they will bring Xikchaka and Zorak within reach of each other," said the *kraan* in its grating, clicking equivalent of human speech. "And then Xikchaka and Zorak may be able to loosen or free each other."

Studying the manner of the petals, the Tharkoonian perceived what had already become obvious to the coldly logical insect. They were stuck fast to opposite petals, and, always taking into consideration that the petals when fitted together, would match tip to tip, they should then be so close to each other that Zorak with his fingers could pluck and tear loose the tendrils which clung about the many limbs of Xikchaka, while the insect-creature, for his part, could do the same for Zorak, using his pincers, claw-tipped mandibles, and other members in lieu of hands.

There was, then, nothing to be done before nightfall. The long, weary day dragged with interminable slowness toward its end. For the beginning period of his imprisonment, Zorak had nourished within his heart the hope that Niamh the Fair would fly the sky-craft down to effect his rescue. Since this had not as yet occurred, and as more

than a few hours had passed since he had fallen into the
clutches of the predatory flower, obviously something had
interfered with her freedom of action. Or, quite simply,
she did not possess the knowledge or skills required to pilot the flying vessel.

It did not, as it happened, even occur to Zorak that the
Princess of Phaolon thought him fallen into the abyss and
long since dead. From the position in which he was helplessly bound, he could not clearly see the great branch
far above them, for if he had been able to observe its
position, he would have realized that from the edge of the
branch above him the girl simply could not see the great
flower where it grew.

Night fell, black winged, smothering the light. As the
huge red ant had predicted, the petals of the monstrous
cannibal flower began to close together. They moved jerk-
ily and in random spasms, but it was obvious to the stalwart bowman that soon he and the *kraan* would be face
to face.

They had only a short time to set each other free, or
both would smother in the thick, clinging maw of the
man-eating monster.

Then the blossom closed, and suddenly Zorak found
himself gasping for breath.

At the same moment he felt the cold touch of the
kraan's jaws grasping for his throat.

Had the skies of the Green Star World been eyed with
stars instead of veiled behind perpetual mists, they might,
after a time, have observed an unusual and unprecedented
sight.

From a long rent torn in the underside of a monstrous
flower there issued slowly and weakly into the open air
the form of a man. From head to foot his body was
smeared with a sticky fluid. His limbs and torso were
scored with abrasions and bruises, but he lived and
seemed uninjured.

Reaching back into the heart of the torn blossom, he helped another creature forth into the air. It was a gigantic scarlet insect, like a huge red ant grown to the size of a hippopotamus.

Despite its mighty proportions, this second creature to emerge from the throat of the vampire blossom moved feebly, its many jointed limbs twitching erratically, its chitin-clad form glistening with the slobber of the man-killing plant.

Man and insect helped each other farther up the surface of the mighty branch to which the flower, now wilting, fluids leaking from the long tear in its throat, clung with many rootlets.

For the first time in the long history of this strange and wondrous world of many marvels and mysteries, a child of the race of men had found an unlikely ally with one of the cold, logical, merciless *kraan.*

And for the first time since the evolution of their races, a member of the *kraan* hordes had an inkling of the meaning of a great and noble and very beautiful word: friendship.

8.

Escape to Peril

They spent that night together upon the great branch, nestling in the hollow socket from which a small bough had once protruded, burrowing among dead leaves.

Every instinct in the heart of Zorak the Bowman urged him to quit the company of the *kraan*, but the Tharkoonian closed his ears to those inner urgings and remained in proximity to Xikchaka. Although the ant and human were natural enemies, the huge insect-creature was greatly debilitated by his captivity in the toils of the cannibal flower and could hardly propel himself along the branch. Obviously, the great ant had been imprisoned in the blossom for days without food or drink.

Zorak assisted the *kraan* to the hollow place in the branch, then reconnoitered to find food and water. He found water in a natural cistern—one of the dead leaves which, dry and tightly curled, was as long as a canoe. He also found a giant acorn shell in which he carried water to the helpless *kraan*. For food he came upon and killed one of the immense tree-snails, whose tender meat sufficed for both of them.

The *kraan* accepted these ministrations without comment; but it was easy to see that he found the actions of Zorak baffling. At length, his hunger and thirst satisfied, the great insect spoke.

"Why does Zorak tend to Xikchaka in this manner?"

inquired the *kraan* in his rasping, clicking approximation of human speech.

"Why not?" returned the bowman. "Xikchaka is weak and feeble, and will die if not tended. Since we assisted each other in freeing ourselves from the embrace of the murderous blossom, shall not our friendship continue?"

" 'Friendship,' " repeated Xikchaka, as if meditating on the word. "This is one of the words in the language of the manlings for which the *kraan* know no meaning."

"The others being 'love,' 'kindness,' and 'mercy,' I imagine." Zorak smiled. The insect-creature regarded him with a cold, unblinking gaze.

"Quite correct," he clacked. "The race of Zorak and the race of Xikchaka are natural foes; why, then, does Zorak not abandon Xikchaka to his own fate?"

"You might as well ask why we helped each other to escape from the grip of the scarlet tendrils," said the bowman.

"Not so," countered the *kraan*. "That was only logical. Alone, neither Zorak nor Xikchaka could have effected their escape. In order for either to survive, both had to work together in unison. Xikchaka's kind understand the meaning of cooperation, but the meaning of 'friendship' eludes us."

Zorak regarded his companion in misfortune with something very like sympathy in his expression. How to explain the warmer emotions to a creature which functioned according to cold, merciless logic? He decided to try.

"Our races may be natural enemies, as you say," he remarked. "But that law does not necessarily extend to each and every individual member of the race. In extraordinary circumstances, even natural foes forget their enmity. If Xikchaka has ever seen a fire in the great trees, he will recall that in the presence of a greater danger, even the rabbit and the fox forget their roles as hunted and hunter, and flee from the fire side by side."

Of course, Zorak did not speak of rabbits and foxes, but of their Laonese equivalents. The sense of his remark was as I have given it here, however.

Xikchaka pondered this in silence for a time.

"If Xikchaka does not understand friendship, or the feeling of sympathy one intelligent creature may experience in regarding the sufferings or the helplessness of another, perhaps he will be able to comprehend the sheer logic of survival," said the Tharkoonian after a time.

"How is that?" asked the insect-creature.

"Together, we stand twice as good a chance of surviving in the wilderness, as either of us would enjoy were we alone."

Xichaka pondered this; then he twitched his antennae in the *kraan* equivalent of a shrug.

"Perhaps. But it is not logical that we should assist each other, no matter what Zorak says," was the only comment the great insect had to make. After a time, he added: "However, if Zorak wishes to persist in his illogical behavior, Xikchaka desires to quench his thirst again."

Zorak grinned, chuckled, shook his head, and gave it up as hopeless. Then he went back to get more water for his weird companion in peril.

The unspoken truce between them lasted into the next day. When dawn lit up the world of the giant trees, Zorak arose and discovered that the *kraan* had recovered the better part of his strength. They journeyed down the branch together, going single file. There was little conversation between the two.

Zorak had torn off some of the fleshy meat from the tree-snail on which they had dined, and bore it with him, wrapped in a segment of leaf. Until they encountered more edible prey, this small store must suffice to assuage their hunger.

He dearly regretted the loss of his bow and arrows, for without them he was unarmed and virtually helpless, at the mercy of whatever predatory beast or reptile might come upon them. Nature had armed Xikchaka with a tough body-armor and with dagger-sharp mandibles, but the divinity had not been so thoughtful in the case of the Tharkoonian. As they progressed down the branch toward the mountainous trunk of the arboreal colossus, the bowman kept his eyes peeled for something which could be employed as a weapon. He had in mind the stinger of a dead wasp, or a javelin-long thorn perhaps, but found neither.

In case they were attacked, his only hope was that Xikchaka would fight on his behalf. Alone, friendless, and unarmed, the human inhabitants of the giant forest were the most helpless of creatures. Somehow, he felt an inner certainty that the insect-creature would fight for him in event of battle. But he could not be sure of this.

With a shrug, Zorak resigned himself philosophically to the whims of fate. The stalwart Tharkoonian saw no profit in worrying over possible events whose occurrence he could foresee but neither avoid nor influence. He resolved to take things as they came. In simple fact, he had no other choice.

By midday they reached the fork of the branch. Here it joined itself to the bole of the enormous tree. They could go no farther.

The *kraan,* with his multiple limbs, could easily descend the trunk to a lower branch, or ascend to a higher. Zorak, however, would find the going a bit more difficult. Luckily, the bark of the tree-trunk was rough and scaly, affording the Tharkoonian a variety of hand- and foot-holds. Beneath them, about a quarter of a mile below their present height, a truly gigantic branch grew from the trunk and extended for some two miles across the gap between this tree and the next. The world-forest was so thickly grown in this coastal region, that they could actually travel afoot between the trees for very considerable distances.

Zorak's inclination was, however, to ascend to the branch above and attempt to discover the fate of Niamh the Fair. He trusted to find the sky craft of Ralidux moored to the branch above. He attempted to convey this to Xikchaka, but the ant did not understand why the human should care in the least as to the fate of the female, and had utterly no comprehension of a machine that could fly. Xikchaka wanted to descend, and Zorak to travel in the opposite direction.

Here, then, their paths must part.

However, this was not fated to occur.

Zorak bade farewell to his traveling companion, who made no reply. Then the Tharkoonian began to climb the tree-trunk. It was slow going, and would probably have been impossible to such as you or me, to climb a vertical surface some two miles above the world's bottom, clinging to minute interstices with toes and fingers alone. Luckily, the human inhabitants of the World of the Green Star are immune to vertigo. Even so, Zorak's climb was made at a slow rate, for the ascent was more difficult than it looked.

He did not get far.

Suddenly, a great red ant was above him, and two others clung to the trunk on either side. Looking down at the branch he had left, he saw and recognized Xikchaka amid a number of his fellow *kràan*.

The other insect-creatures had apparently just ascended to the branch on which he and Xikchaka had spent the hours of darkness. It was equally obvious to Zorak that the other creatures were warrior-ants from the same horde as Xikchaka, for Xikchaka was not engaged in fighting them but seemed to be communicating with his fellows in some telepathic manner. The *kraan* he had assisted in escaping from the clutches of the cannibal flower did not seem in the slightest to be concerned that Zorak was about to be captured.

Clinging spread-eagled against the bark, Zorak was helpless to fight off his attackers. They plucked him from his place and bore him down the trunk to the fork of the branch.

Then, after the rapid exchange of more silent signals or some manner of communication between themselves, the *kraan* warparty, bearing their helpless human captive, began descending the trunk to the lower bough.

As they came within clear view of the mighty branch below, Zorak saw a sight which plunged him into the depths of gloom.

The branch was aswarm with literally thousands of the *kraan*.

Hope died within his breast at the sight. From a few of the giant insects, he might perhaps have won free by trick or luck or daring. But from amid the full number of the scarlet horde, a hundred men could not have battled to freedom.

A tether was looped about his throat by nimble mandibles. In no time he was added to the end of a line of Laonese captives. They were a ragged, half-starved, dispirited lot, and their woeful, cowed condition did not bode well for the immediate future of Zorak the Bowman. But that was not what bothered him: it was that Xikchaka paid not the slightest heed to his predicament, nor even deigned to look at him.

Enslaved to the ant horde, Zorak was led off with the other captives down the great branch.

9.

Preparations for War

Zorak the Bowman soon discovered the meaning of slavery. The *kraan* horde had many human captives, and among these he found men from several of the treetop cities. There were slaves from Kamadhong and from Ardha, the city of Akhmim the Tyrant where once Zarqa and Janchan and I had labored to rescue Niamh the Fair. There were even among the captives of the ant-army men from Niamh's own city, Phaolon.

Some were hunters seized while far from their accustomed place; others were the survivors of war parties which had been attacked by the *kraan*; still others had been peaceful merchants, travelers, or traders en route between various of the Laonese cities.

There were even a certain number of forest outlaws—the homeless exiles, driven from their cities for one or another criminal offense, who had made a new home amid the wilderness of giant trees. Some, as well, were forest savages taken in war. There were many such tribes of primitive barbarians who dwelt in the giant trees; I, Karn, was one of these last.

It puzzled Zorak that the ant-army should bother taking captives at all, or, having taken them, that the red ant warriors should bother keeping them alive. But the stalwart bowman from far Tharkoon soon stumbled upon the reason for this peculiarly un-antlike behavior trait. The

66

insect-creatures, although of considerable intelligence and admirably suited by nature to their environment, lacked certain skills which only their human slaves possessed.

The problem lay in the very nature of the *kraan*, as opposed to human beings. I have described the insect-creatures as red ants grown to enormous proportions, and this indeed they were. A scientist of my native world, given the opportunity to study the *kraan*, might notice differences in anatomical details between the *kraan* and their minuscule Terrestrial cousins. But whether or not they were true ants down to the smallest detail, or merely resembled the Earthly insects so closely as to seem antlike to the untutored eye, is a matter of trifling importance. They were more antlike than not.

Now ants have multiple limbs, and these limbs terminate in mandibular extremities. However cunningly nature has devised these mandibles, they simply are not of the same construction as human hands. The *kraan*, therefore, are unable to manipulate objects with the degree of manual dexterity of which human beings are capable. Our hands, with their swivel-socket wrists and opposing thumbs, are uniquely designed for the use of tools. The mandibles of the *kraan* are not.

But the *kraan* were of sufficient intelligence to be tool-making and tool-using creatures. Their coldly logical minds were aware of the advantages afforded to those races which are equipped by nature to employ the use of tools and weapons. Lacking the ability to use instruments more sophisticated than mere sticks or poles limited the skills of the *kraan* and put them at a disadvantage compared to their principal enemies and rivals for dominance—which is to say, the race of men.

By themselves, the *kraan* were unable to control their environment. But through the use of human captives, whose skills were at the service of their insect masters, the *kraan* were as dangerous to the men of the treetop cities as they were to each other.

It had become the custom of the ant-army to take as many human captives as possible, and these slaves were employed in a variety of skilled crafts. They kept records and made mathematical computations for their insect masters; they devised tools and weapons adapted, wherever possible, to the structure of the *kraan* mandibles. They scraped the hides and intestines of beasts for the manufacture of bowstrings and catapult cables, manufactured a variety of sword-blades, spear-points, knives and daggers; and in all ways served the *kraan* in those areas of endeavor for which nature had inadequately suited the limbs of the warrior ants.

Zorak was new to the treetop world, for his native city, Tharkoon, was built upon a spur of land which jutted out into the blue waters of the Komarian Sea. His race was a nation of landsmen who tilled the soil and fished the seas. The unique perils and protections afforded to those of the Laonese who dwelt a mile or more aloft on the branches of the arboreal giants were matters upon which the bowman had never before found reason to ponder. But even he, as inexperienced in this setting as he was, could realize the enormous menace the *kraan* represented to the tree kingdoms.

On their own, the giant insects were fearsome and dreaded opponents. Armored entirely in tough, horny chitin, they were shielded from the bows and spears of human armies. With a logical, unemotional intelligence comparable to that of the human brain, they were as cunning and skillful tacticians as were their human foes. Armed with sharp clawlike extremities, bristling with powerful many-jointed limbs, each ant warrior could hold at bay three or even four human soldiers.

But when, to these inherent advantages, was added a full use of the crafts and skills possible to their human slaves, the scarlet horde became a double threat to the survival of the kingdoms of men.

It was not a pleasant thought to think upon, and the

sleep of Zorak that first night was troubled by dark and ominous dreams.

During the next day the brave bowman struck up a friendship with one of the smiths, a burly-chested fellow who called himself Xargo of Kamadhong. The smith told Zorak that he had been captured by the horde about a year ago, as nearly as he could measure the passage of time, which was without any particular accuracy, as I have elsewhere explained.*

Xargo had been employed all this while, he told Zorak, in the manufacture of sword-blades and spear-tips, and in the making of arrowheads. Quite a considerable number of the other slaves of the *kraan* were employed in similar warlike manufacture, very many of which captives Xargo himself had taught the art of smithery. He began to instruct Zorak in the requisite skills, for it was the goal of the leader of the horde that every *kraan* in the giant army should be fully equipped for war.

The Laonese manufacture metals, but do not mine for ore. The only exception to this practice may be the Komarian isles and seacoast cities, but I cannot say for certain. At any rate, in lieu of bronze, copper, iron, or steel—all of which metals can only be obtained by surface or subsurface mining—the Laonese employ a peculiar

---

* In several places the author of these narratives has expounded on the odd lack of interest the Laonese take in chronology. They in no way measure the lapse of intervals of time as we do. People on the Green Star World do not divide time into weeks or months, and seem to have no system by which years are measured. They have, therefore, no idea of their own individual age. This would seem to be only natural on a world in which there is no seasonal variation in temperature and from which neither moon nor stars can be seen. The Laonese obtuseness on this topic is further compounded by the fact that, because of their aerial habitations, most of the Laonese civilizations do not plant, harvest, or subsist on crops. The only Laonese cultures which do employ agriculture are the denizens of the coastal cities about the Komarian Sea, such as Zorak's own kingdom.   —*Editor.*

transparent metal like glass hardened to the toughness, the resilience, and the sharpness of steel.

In the treetop cities, these metals are derived from the sap of the giant trees by a method of chemical distilling for which I can find in the English language no precise equivalent. Metals are held in suspension within the sap of the forest giants, and are "grown" in molds like some manner of organic crystals. I have never actually seen this done, due to the brevity of my stay in any of the Laonese cities I have yet visited, and therefore cannot describe with more precision just how it is accomplished. But, however the thing is done, Xargo soon began teaching the skills to Zorak, on instruction of the insect-creatures.

In conversation with the master-smith, Zorak discovered that the armament program had only very recently been accelerated to a new pitch. Xargo explained that only recently the king or chieftain of the ant horde had given orders that the team of smiths was to quadruple its endeavors.

When Zorak inquired as to the reason of the king-ant—a ferocious-looking giant insect whose name was Rkhith—Xargo looked thoughtful.

"Rkhith has taken a human slave only shortly before you yourself were made prisoner," growled the burly smith. "He must be a very clever man, this new slave, for he has risen overnight to a position of considerable authority over his fellow captives. In fact, he has the ear of Rkhith himself, if I may use the term in respect to a creature who has no such organs of hearing!"

"And what does this new slave have to do with arming the insect horde?" asked Zorak.

The smith shrugged truculently. "Only the Gods know," he growled. "But scuttlebutt in the slave-pens has it that this fellow is a turncoat, a cunning renegade who would lead the *kraan* against the treetop cities. He seems to have painted such an alluring picture of the wealth and lavish possessions of one forest kingdom in particular, that for the first time in all their history the red ant horde will soon attempt to conquer one of the cities of men. It is for this reason that the horde is being armed with every available weapon, and with such speed as we smiths can perform our tasks."

"What city do you refer to?" inquired Zorak.

"Phaolon," replied the smith.

A day or two after this conversation, Zorak had the opportunity to see for himself the traitorous turncoat who would guide the insect horde against the fairest of the cities of men.

The chance came during a tour of inspection that afternoon, when Rkhith came in person to observe the progress Xargo's men had made with the new "crop" of weapons.

The insect warlord was a veritable monster of his kind, his armored thorax adorned with sparkling gems and plates of precious metals, for all the world like a human conqueror.

Amid the warlord's sizable retinue of *kraan* guards and the elite of the warrior ants walked only one human being. He was a slender man of sensitive, even aristocratic mien, and one of indeterminate age.

For all that he was a member of the human species, which the *kraan* despised as inferior to their own kind, he went clad in silken raiment very unlike the filthy rags worn by the other slaves of the horde.

Even more oddly, his skin was a distinct and unusual color. Most of the Laonese races have complexions which range from tawny or sallow yellow to the hues of parchment or old ivory. But the pigmentation of Rkhith's favorite personal slave was an odd and rare color. He was *blue*.

As the giant king-ant came crawling down the double row of sword-blade casting vats, the human workers bent busily over their tasks.

None bent lower or seemed busier than Zorak of Tharkoon.

The fumes of the seething chemical froth served to veil his features, and as he bent over the vat with his back turned to the crawling monster insect, Zorak hoped that no one in Rkhith's retinue would take any notice of him. The reason for this was that the silk-clad slave who strolled casually at Rkhith's side might well have recognized Zorak had he seen his face.

For Zorak had seen *his* face, and knew him instantly.

It was Delgan.

10.

On the March

For days thereafter, the insect-creatures kept Xargo and his assistants busy night and day at the crystal breeding vats. The manufacture of weapons, however, was a process that could not be hurried, which did not exactly please Rkhith; however, there was nothing within the power of the ant warlord which might accelerate the procedures of nature.

Daily the red ant warriors practiced with their new weapons, while gradually marching in what Zorak correctly presumed to be the direction of Phaolon. Clasping spears or swords in their forelimbs, the enormous chitin-mailed creatures made the most formidable opponents imaginable. Zorak grimly lamented the destiny of Phaolon, or of any of the other cities of men unfortunate enough to attract the enmity of the scarlet horde.

But there was nothing he could do about it.

From conversations he had overheard back on the isle of Komar, the Tharkoonian archer was well aware that Niamh the Fair was the hereditary Princess of Phaolon. He had never seen or even visited the Jewel City himself, for the distances between his native Tharkoon and the treetop city were considerable, and between the several realms of the Green Star World there is little commerce. But he was aware that Prince Janchan also hailed from Phaolon, and that Janchan, together with his new bride,

Arjala, Karn the Hunter, and Zarqa the Kalood, had for
some time past endeavored to find the lost girl in order to
restore her to her kingdom.

Now, it seemed, the kingdom itself would be lost—in a
somewhat different sense—before they managed to restore
Niamh to her throne.

The bowman knew that his former comrades would be
intensely concerned, could he only communicate his discoveries to them. This, of course, was doubly impossible,
or, at least, unlikely. The one reason being his own immo-
bilization, for slaves and prisoners by very definition have
no freedom of movement. The other being that he did not
know the whereabouts of his former friends.

Since they had entered the world-forest in the sky-ship
of Ralidux, and since he had by accident been separated
from Niamh the Fair, Zorak had lost all sense of direction. It is quite difficult to ascertain direction on the
World of the Green Star under the best of circumstances,
as I have elsewhere noted, but once within the forest of
enormous trees—each of which looks interchangeable
with the next—it is all but impossible. Ever since the ant
army had made him a captive, and had forced him to accompany the horde on its crawling march, Zorak had become thoroughly disoriented.

The Tharkoonian bowman was a thoughtful, resourceful man, and not at all the sort to yield supinely to what
seemed an inevitable fate. Although he was held a
prisoner by the horde of warrior *kraan*, he never ceased
to contemplate the possibilities for an escape to freedom.
During the long days and nights while he labored at the
metallurgical vats, Zorak discussed their situation with his
fellow captives. Some of these had been enslaved for so
long to the *kraan* that they had become dispirited, losing
all hope of ever being free again. Others, however, yet
nurtured in their hearts the burning desire for freedom.

"Yours is not the first voice that has been raised in
hopes of escape," a grim-faced Ardhanese informed

Zorak. "In the many years I have been a prisoner of the *kraan*, more than a few have tried to make a break for freedom."

"Have any yet succeeded?" Zorak asked.

The heavy-faced Ardhanese shook his head.

"Our situation is peculiarly helpless," he observed in a somber tone. "We are not held captive in a city, but in the wilderness itself. We are surrounded by many thousands of alert and vigilant warrior *kraan*, who are continually on the move from one branch to another, or from one tree to another. At any given moment of night or day, literally hundreds of ant scouts range far afield in all directions, alert to give warning to the central body of the horde in case of the approach of enemies. It is not a matter of jailbreak, which is a comparatively simple matter, but of eluding hundreds of scouts who might be anywhere or everywhere about us."

Zorak nodded thoughtfully, storing this opinion away in his mind to ponder upon later. He soon came to realize the peculiar difference between this sort of imprisonment, by a mobile force, and imprisonment in a stationary place. There was also the unique problem of being held captive by the warrior ants. For had he been enslaved by an enemy city, once free the bowman could have mingled with the inhabitants of the city and lost himself in their number, since they were human beings like himself, and racial or national origins are largely indistinguishable on this world. But a human held captive by the scarlet ant horde is uniquely vulnerable. He does not in any way resemble his captors, and each of the *kraan* knows at a glance that any human it may encounter is an enemy and a slave. Escape to freedom, then, became a very different kind of problem.

The horde progressed on forced daily marches through the sky-tall forest, growing ever nearer and nearer to unsuspecting Phaolon. The ant warriors became increasingly familiar and expert in the use of the weapons manufactured by Xargo and his assistants.

Many times during the march Zorak saw Delgan from afar, but the traitorous blue man was always amid the retinue of the king-ant and did not seem to observe or to recognize the Tharkoonian bowman.

On more than one occasion, Zorak encountered his former fellow captive, Xikchaka. Generally, this occurred during one or another of the errands he performed at the request of the master-smith. On none of these occasions did he have the opportunity to exchange any words with Xikchaka—not that he felt particularly inclined to exchange polite words with the *kraan* he had rescued and tended, and who had then betrayed him into the captivity of the horde.

The motives of Xikchaka in this act of betrayal were quite beyond the imagination of the bowman. Men such as he prize the bond of friendship, loyalty, and comradeship beyond most other allegiances. Zorak would far rather have betrayed his allegiance to Prince Parimus, or to the city of Tharkoon itself, rather than betray a friend.

He was aware that concepts such as loyalty and friendship between comrades were alien to the emotionless mentality of the *kraan,* and therefore he could not exactly come to hate Xikchaka, who remained true to the instincts of his kind. The *kraan,* like the Earthly insects they so closely resemble in all matters save that of size, share the so-called hive mentality. They are not so much individual entities as they are units in a group or community. To that community they owe primary obligations which vastly outweigh individual whim or debt or inclination. It is like the difference between a slave state and a free republic: in the slave state, the individual exists only to serve the state, and his personal inclinations are of distinctly secondary importance; but in the true republic, the state exists primarily to serve the individual, whose first obligation is to himself. So Zorak could hardly blame the cold, emotionless *kraan* for what seemed to him a betrayal: their friendship had been too brief, it seemed, for him to have taught the warrior ant the meaning of that noble and beautiful word—"friendship."

As the horde approached the outskirts of that portion of the world-forest under the dominance of Phaolon, the *kraan* began taking extraordinary precautions to avoid premature discovery by the Phaolonese.

Chevaliers of Phaolon, mounted on fleet-winged *zaiph*, ranged as scouts over that portion of the forest which lay in proximity to the Jewel City, ever alert to danger. The ant horde concealed itself as best it could during the hours when the Green Star was aloft, and only under cover of darkness did the horde advance toward the city of Niamh the Fair.

It was an uncanny experience to Zorak. By night, when the moonless gloom lay thick and unbroken upon the whispering forest, the chittering and rustling horde of monster insects poured like a crawling tide down the branches of the great trees, with the human captives borne helplessly along amid the flowing wave of insect-creatures.

Security was at a maximum pitch now, and vigilant ant sentries kept careful watch on the slave population.

The only hope the human captives had for making a break for freedom lay either in the moment of attack upon the city, when the ant horde would be otherwise engaged and much too busy to watch over their slaves, or in some unexpected diversion which might occur between the present moment and the attack.

What this diversion might be, Zorak had no way of guessing in advance. But he watched and waited, and so did his fellow captives. Even those who had been imprisioned so long they had grown apathetic became infected with Zorak's determination for escape. The humans whispered among themselves and laid their plans with care, largely ignored by the *kraan*, who held men in contempt and considered themselves to be the evolutionary superiors of humanity.

Zorak believed that such a diversion could come at any moment, and organized the captives to be ever on the alert and ready to strike boldly for freedom when the diversion came.

Day broke, and the ant horde concealed itself on the underside of the gigantic branch, or hid motionless beneath thick canopies of verdure.

Night fell, and the horde marched upon Phaolon.

And then came the moment for which Zorak had so long waited.

The Third Book

IN THE
OPAL TOWER

11.

Karn in Chains

The girl savages, who had found me asleep in the sky-sled and had made me their captive, had their camp far out on a branch of the mighty tree, where several smaller branchlets diverged from the central bough.

Here leaves sprouted in thick clouds of tissue-of-gold, forming a screen which effectively shielded their settlement from chance scrutiny.

The camp itself was an exceedingly ingenious complex of huts and cabins built on several levels, and connected by aerial walkways and rope-bridges, with porches and verandas roofed by leaf-bearing twigs cunningly bent awry, and all manner of ladders and steps leading from one level to another. All of these structures were built of the same wood as the branches themselves, which served as additional camouflage to conceal the existence of the camp from the eyes of enemies bestial or human.

The wild girls had stripped me to the buff in order to amuse themselves by shaming and humiliating me, but I endured my captivity and their scorn with whatever stoicism I could muster.

Wearying at length of making sport of me, my mistress, the thirteen-year-old hoyden they called Varda, assigned me to menial tasks. I was set to work scrubbing the cook-pots and cleaning the acorn-cup dishes and other kitchen implements, and at mealtimes I brought food to the tables where the girls ate.

As nearly as I could tell there were twenty or more of the Amazon girls in the encampment. As I came to know them better, I decided that Varda's chief rival for the chieftainship, the girl called Iona, was probably older than the rest, being at most fifteen. I have elsewhere described Iona, but I will reiterate by saying that she was not tall for her age, but more firmly fleshed and a bit more voluptuous of bosom, hips, and thighs than the other, mostly younger, girls of the band. Her skin was the color of old parchment, and she had huge eyes of tawny amber, and floating hair of thistledown-silver. Unlike the littler girls, who scampered about naked except for a bit of hide twisted about their loins, she went decently covered.

Varda, the girl who "owned" me, was about two years her junior, a snub-nosed, wide-mouthed, freckle-faced young tomboy with supple, nimble limbs and a firm if shallow bosom inadequately covered by the tanned hide she wore strapped about her with thongs. Whereas Varda treated me scornfully, brusquely ordering me about and gleefully seizing upon every conceivable excuse to punish me or insult me, Iona bore an ill-concealed hatred of me, seemingly because I was of the male sex, with no other reason ever enunciated. Iona would have killed me had she dared, but Varda and the other girls wished to keep me alive if only as something to bully and mistreat.

The girl savages lived in the most slovenly manner imaginable, rarely washed, argued constantly, and fought incessantly. They slept, for the most part, in hammocks out in the open, but some of the younger children, the nine or ten-year-old girls, shared cabins and slept in nests of furs.

I slept on a rude pallet in a tiny lean-to attached to Varda's hut, which was larger and more comfortably fitted out with furniture than the rest of the living quarters.

When there was no cooking or washing up to do, I was sent out to gather food. This consisted in the main of nuts, berries, fruit, and a species of immense and edible mushroom which grew on the underside of one of the larger network of branches of the network that comprised the camp area. The Amazon girls usually went out hunting during the day, seeking the tender and enormous grubs, insect larvae, the defenseless and delicious tree-snails, and other easily killed varieties of game with which the upper terraces of the great trees teemed.

When on my expeditions to gather nuts and berries, I wore a choke halter around my neck and was only permitted out in the care of five or six of the little girls, who kept me constantly tethered. They would scamper about, dangling head down from the branch, or, perched in a row, sit kicking their heels, while I climbed gingerly down to the end of the twiglets and slowly, one by one, picked the nuts. These were like walnuts, but of the size of basketballs, and contained several pounds of delectable nut-meat. The berries grew from plant parasites which sprouted from some of the branches, their fruit resembling that of the strawberry.

The naked little imps delighted in shouting abuse at me, and tugged at my leash until they nearly throttled me, while giggling at my discomfort or my nakedness; probably at both. For some reason they took a particularly vicious pleasure in tormenting me. Before long I found out why.

I learned that they had been taken from their homes by a slave raid about nine months ago (insofar as it was possible to compute the passage of time). Their homes had been on the outskirts of one of the treetop cities previously unknown to me, a place called Barganath. The slavers had seized them for training and sale to the brothels of some of the other Laonese cities, and from the jabber I overheard, I got the impression that the girl-children had been abused and molested by their captors. From this mistreatment obviously stemmed their hatred and loathing of males, which was quite understandable, although it did not help me to endure with equanimity the humiliation and punishment I suffered at their hands.

It was Varda who had led their escape. The older girl had taken advantage of a sudden attack by *zzumalak* on the slavers' camp. The *zzumalak* are honeybees, but honeybees grown to the size and proportion of tigers, and every bit as dangerous. While the slavers rallied to fight off the assault by these flying predators, Varda had led the girls to freedom. They had caught one of the slavers off guard, seized his keys, unlocked their cages, and swarmed over the men, pulling them down with nails and teeth and whatever weapons they managed to snatch up. Caught between the attacking *zzumalak* an⁄ the attacking girls, the slavers had died to the last man.

Having cut down to the last man the brutal slavers, and now having won their freedom, the band of girls found themselves hopelessly lost amid the worldwide forest of gigantic trees. They had not the slightest idea in which direction the city of Barganath might lie, nor how distant it might be from the point to which the slaver-caravan had carried them. This was largely because the caravan had traveled mostly by night, and for the beginning of the journey the captive girls had been bound and gagged and blindfolded in the bargain.

On the planet of the Green Star there are no signposts, and very few maps.

Since to find their way back home to Barganath was a hopeless endeavor, the girls simply wandered for a time until they came at last to this twig-ridden part of the branch, where a natural hiding place among the twists and nooks of the branchlets offered a safe haven to them.

And here they stayed.

It had been the quick-witted and aggressive Varda who had first seized upon the moment of the attack of the *zzumalak* swarm as the most propitious time for their attempted escape. And it had been Varda who had realized and pointed out the many advantages their present camp-site offered to them. For these reasons, and because of her natural talent for leadership, the girls had elected the thirteen-year-old as their leader.

This, it seemed, did not sit well with Iona. Since she was older than Varda, she thought the captaincy should have fallen to her. Iona was perfectly happy to let some-one else do the dirty work of making plans, giving deci-sions, and working up the ways in which things were to be done. But she heartily disliked the idea of someone else giving orders to *her*—especially a younger girl, less mature, less developed, who in her eyes was her inferior.

But the rest of the band were pleased with the way Varda managed things, and disliked Iona, who was al-ways sulking and criticizing and bearing grudges. Besides, Iona bossed and bullied the little girls—that is, whenever Varda or one of the other older girls were not around.

Iona bided her time; she did not seem to have much chance in capturing the leadership of the savage band from her hated rival. She schemed and planned and tried to ingratiate those girls she could not intimidate; and in-timidate those who were not amenable to her form of flat-tery. She watched and listened for any morsel of gossip she could find to use as a weapon against those she could neither browbeat nor cajole.

In particular, she kept her eyes on Varda.

If she could catch Varda in some infraction of the code by which they lived, if she could discover Varda breaking one of her own rules, then Iona thought she would have a potent weapon with which to dislodge her rival from the position of power Iona so dearly coveted.

It made for a lot of tension and mutual dislike and sus-picion between the two older girls.

Iona regarded Varda with poorly concealed envy and was always quick to question the wisdom of her decisions, and Varda regarded Iona with amusement and more than a bit of contempt which she did not even try to hide. In a way, the rivalry between these two was like a tug-of-war.

I soon found myself in the most uncomfortable spot imaginable—right in the middle!

12.

Beyond the Portal

The mysterious tower that Niamh discovered rose from the branch and soared aloft many stories into the green-gold dimness. It did not resemble any similar structure built by men, or at least none known to the experience of the Princess of Phaolon.

The spire seemed made from some smooth, sleek ceramic, like porcelain, and to have been made all of one piece. At least no joints were discernible to the eye. The graceful, fluid curves of its architecture were as unfamiliar to the girl as was the substance from which it was fashioned. This substance shimmered with changing hues, like some unthinkably enormous opal: dim rose and fiery gold, shot through with glint of copper green and peacock blue, fading at times to nacreous pearl or darkening to wrathful crimson. The shifting hues seemed obedient to some stimulus other than reflective light. The girl was intrigued, puzzled, and fascinated. She was not, to any particular extent, frightened.

The girl approached the curious structure. It gave the impression of extreme age, of unthinkably remote antiquity. It also somehow conveyed to her the feeling that it was unoccupied, and had been unoccupied for a very long time.

Had Niamh seen the Pylon of Sarchimus the Wise, as I had, it is likely that the princess would have recognized

87

the Opal Tower as closely similar in structure, design, and material to that one.

Sarchimus had dwelt in a dead city called Sotaspra, which had formerly been inhabited by the Kaloodha, an all-but-extinct race of gaunt, gold-skinned, telepathically gifted Winged Men. They had been the masters of an amazing science, the Kaloodha, but a form of racial madness drove them to suicide. The lust for immortality was the fata morgana which had lured them over the brink of destruction. Today, only Zarqa alone was left of his vanished people. But their enigmatic handiwork could still be found here and there about the Green Star World. Their towers and cities had been built to last, and they had indeed lasted, untouched by time, for countless hundreds of millenia.

The Opal Tower suggested to Niamh a long-ago abandonment. Not that the sleek, glowing, glassy stone from which the tower was built had suffered from the merciless erosion of the ages. Quite to the contrary, no chip or crack or sign of crumbling could Niamh discern in all the luminous fabric of the shining structure. But an aura of emptiness clung about it like the reek of death and decay, all but palpable.

So, albeit warily, the girl approached the soaring spire.

The ever-changing colors that crawled and swirled across the gliding lines of the tower lent it the illusion of inner life, which formed an uncanny contrast with the air of abandonment and emptiness that pervaded its proximity. The princess noticed that the sleek, soaring curves of the wall were unbroken by any windows. The portal, however, when she came within sight of it, stood open: a tall, narrow, tapering entrance with a broad base and dwindling sides that grew together at the pointed top.

It yawned like an orifice, like a sphincter or a maw. Open, inviting, unguarded.

For a moment, Niamh lingered on the threshold. A momentary qualm possessed the girl, a trepidation that seemed almost to be trying to warn her against making an entry.

She paused, biting her lip in a torment of indecision.

The Opal Tower afforded her a haven of safety against the predators who would prowl hungrily with the coming of night. And the tower, with its air of seeming neglect and abandonment, was apparently tenantless. Should she go in, or should she pass the tower by?

No pampered exquisite, sheltered from harsh reality, unaccustomed to strife for survival, Niamh was a child of her wilderness world of giant trees and incredible monstrosities. Often before this she had fought for her life against huge odds, and during her long wanderings across the face of the Green Star World she had survived perils beyond number. The staunch girl hefted the bow of Zorak, an arrow nocked and at the ready.

What, after all, was there to fear?

So she approached the yawning portal and entered, and vanished from sight in purple gloom.

The tower closed its doorway, as a patient monster closes its jaws upon its unsuspecting prey.

Where the tapering, pointed entry had been was now a smooth, unbroken surface. It swirled with opalescent hues, that surface. Then it flushed crimson, the color of human blood!

Within the portal, Niamh found herself at one end of a long, winding corridor floored with glassy stuff. The walls soared above her, lost in gloom. Veils of purple shadow thickened about her until she could scarcely see her way and was forced to feel along the wall with one hand, step by step.

Suddenly, the gloom became absolute and the cool breeze which blew against her slender back and shoulders ceased abruptly. Niamh whirled, guessing that the portal was now blocked, that the door which led to freedom and the outer world was no longer open.

With amazement she discovered the portal had ceased

to exist, and that the hallway ended in a slick, unbroken wall.

Then the floor tilted beneath her, curving downward.

With a sharp cry the girl lost her balance and fell forward. Down the steep, smooth incline she shot as down a greased slide.

Ahead of her lay only darkness.

Then the smooth chute down which she slid ended, and the girl hurtled into emptiness.

A resilient, elastic surface broke her fall, driving the air from her lungs. For long moments, gasping for breath, the princess floundered in the folds of some rubbery, yielding stuff, becoming entangled. Gathering her composure, she lay still, peering around her; but the gloom was unbroken.

With admirable foresight, even while falling, Niamh had retained her grip upon Zorak's bow. Now she removed the arrow from the weapon and thrust the sharp metal barb into the elastic fabric which had broken her fall. It ripped and tore, and she sawed away at the rubbery stuff until she had made an opening of some size.

Then, removing from her garment a gem-studded brooch, she dropped the bit of jewelry through the opening, listening until she heard the clink of metal against stone. From the swiftness with which the sound had reached her, Niamh guessed that a stone surface lay not very far beneath her present position.

She dropped five or six feet, landing on a floor of smooth, dry stone.

During the next few moments she carefully felt her way about the dungeon cell into which she had fallen. It was a circular chamber, some ten yards from wall to wall, and completely empty save for herself.

The curving wall was unbroken by any door or entrance, at least at ground level. Feeling her way around the pit, she examined the wall from the floor to as high as she could reach, completely circling the room. She could find no means of escape whatsoever.

After a time, she gave up the attempt, and composed herself upon the floor, against one wall.

The chamber in which she found herself imprisoned resembled a wide stone well.

Unless she could somehow manage to climb back into the rubbery membrane which had caught and broken her fall like a net, and then climb back up through the roof into the corridor again, she was hopelessly imprisoned. And to perform such a feat in complete darkness was not only difficult, it was dangerous.

After a time, she slept. . . .

When she awoke she found a dim radiance now illuminated her cell.

It was seemingly sourceless and seemed to radiate from empty air itself, as if luminous atoms of pure light drifted amid the atmospheric vapors.

By this mysterious and sourceless light, Niamh perceived that the rubbery net had been somehow withdrawn, and that the roof of the circular chamber in which she was captive was something like thirty feet above her. The roof was quite beyond her ability to reach, and now she could perceive no means of exit.

After a time, lacking anything to occupy herself with, the girl fell into a fitful doze again.

When she awoke, she found utensils of crockery laid out near where she lay. There was a green jug filled with cold fresh water, a broad and shallow bowl filled with succulent gobbets of meat swimming in a steamy broth which savored of herbs, and a thick ceramic spoon with which to down the stew.

For a moment, she hesitated to partake of the food, since it was possible that a subtle poison or narcotic had been slipped in it. After a moment's reflection, however, she shrugged aside these fears with a rueful smile.

If her captors wished to kill her, there was no reason for them to supply her with food and drink, she reasoned, and she fell to with a hearty appetite. The stew was delicious, the cold water refreshing. Finishing her meal, the girl set aside the crockery and waited for further developments.

Whatever the reason she had been taken prisoner, at least it was not the intention of her captors to starve her to death, or to drive her mad with thirst.

But they had relieved her of the bow and arrows. . . .

13.

The White Chamber

When next she slept, she woke to find the crockery gone from her side. It became evident to Niamh the Fair that there was some secret entrance into the circular cell besides the mysterious one in the roof.

The roof opening was too far above her head for the princess to make her escape by that route; the other entrance, however, probably lay closer to hand. The courageous, resourceful girl resolved upon a plan to discover its secrets.

During this period of wakefulness, Niamh exercised within her cell, as much to relieve the boredom of her imprisonment as to keep her body in a healthy condition. After she had exercised sufficiently, she lay down a little space from the wall and composed herself as if for slumber.

She closed her eyes, turned over a time or two, then gradually permitted her breathing to become slow and tranquil as if she were indeed sound asleep. But she did not permit herself to slumber, merely feigning it in order to ascertain the method by which her unseen captor entered and left her cell.

Time stretched out, unendurably. The complete relaxation of her body, which was comfortably wearied from her exercises, was insidiously conducive to sleep. The girl determinedly forced herself to stay awake by every means

93

she could think of. She recalled to mind her lineage, ancestor by ancestor, in a chain of descent which stretched back into the remotest ages. She recited mentally the favorite ballads and heroic lays she had years ago committed to memory during her childhood tutoring. She conducted imagined conversations with absent friends, mentally picturing their appearance down to the minutest detail of dress.

After an unendurable time, the faintest sound came to her ears.

It was a mere wisp of a sound, a creaking or rasping, as of stone against stone. Lifting her eyelids very slightly, the girl peered through the fringe of her lashes and observed the smooth, unbroken stone of the circular wall.

Where previously it had been smooth and unbroken, now there existed a straight black line, like a hairline crack, which began at a point about three feet up the wall and extended in a regular line to the place where the floor joined with the bottom of the wall. As she watched breathless with excitement, the crack widened and became a square black opening.

Through this opening now extended a withered hand, like the gaunt, fleshless claw of some monstrous bird!

The hand withdrew, bearing with it the empty crockery which had contained her meal.

Then the black opening began to close in upon itself, but before it had completely closed, Niamh rolled over and thrust a small object into the narrowing opening. It was a thin but tough leather strap torn from her sandal.

The black line shrank to the merest thread. Then all was still. Niamh lay in the same position, still feigning slumber and attempting to make it seem as if her movement had been nothing more than the sort of random stirring a body makes during sleep.

She felt the pressure of unseen eyes upon her as she lay, eyes closed, breathing in and out with long, shallow breaths.

Then the feeling of being watched terminated, and Niamh felt herself to be alone and unobserved once again.

She sat up quickly and examined the wall, probing with the sensitive tips of her fingers. The sandal strap was indeed wedged into the narrowest of openings, which meant that the secret door had not entirely returned to its original position.

This, in turn, suggested that whatever the nature of the locking mechanism which held the door firmly shut, the mechanism might not have fully engaged, due to the slight obstruction. She strove against the seemingly solid wall and pushed and probed, but to no avail.

Taking hold of the end of the strap which protruded from the nearly shut door, Niamh delicately exerted pressure, trying *not* to pull the leather strap from its place but to apply leverage against it, in order to widen the opening.

After a time, the stone door gave a little. Just a little, but enough to spark a flame of hope within the girl's breast.

She then took out the jeweled brooch which she had recovered from the floor of the cell—the same pin she had let fall from the net in order to ascertain the distance to the ground—and began employing this as a tool.

The brooch was in the form of a flat buckle of gilt metal, with a design set in sparkling crystals. The edge of the brooch, however, was just thin enough to enable her to insert it into the crack.

With both hands Niamh now twisted simultaneously at the brooch while tugging on the strap.

After an interminable time, the crack widened still more.

After what seemed like hours of probing and tugging, the girl succeeded in opening the door until it thrust out about one inch from the wall.

Then, using the full strength of her lithe and supple young body, the princess pulled and pulled upon that obtruding edge until her fingers were raw and throbbing with weariness.

But at last the door stood open, revealing an empty square of blackness: into which she crawled headfirst, without a moment's hesitation.

Whatever might lie outside was better than the prison within!

The wall of her cell proved to be about a foot thick. Beyond the secret door she found a corridor that led to a stone staircase which curved up to a higher story of the structure, perhaps at ground level, for it was obvious that she had been imprisoned in some basement level.

Niamh ascended the stair and found an open portal carved of sleek, glistening stone like pale marble.

The chamber into which she peered was lighted with the same sourceless glow of mellow luminosity she had first observed in her cell. But this room was walled with jeweled mosaics in peculiar geometric patterns devoid of any meaning to her. Low taborets and cushioned stools were scattered about, and the gleaming ceramic floor underfoot, colored a brilliant shade of peacock blue, was carpeted with thick, luxurious furs of a creamy hue.

Fur-bearing animals were so rare upon the planet of the Green Star as to be virtually unknown, but Niamh entered the room without giving thought to this minor mystery. Where all is unknown, so trivial an enigma is unworthy of notice.

In the opposite wall yawned another doorway, hung with a curtain composed of glassy beads—red, blue, amber yellow—strung on long cords. Through this curtain she could see another room, a larger room, with a domed ceiling. It was filled with complicated apparatus whose purposes were not known to her, yet it was untenanted, so the girl shouldered through the curtain and stepped within.

A sharp medicinal stench bit her nostrils—the piercing

odor of disinfectant. She gained the center of the domed chamber, and gazed about her with some perplexity.

The walls were lined with metal cabinets with glass doors and shelves covered with glittering bladed implements that looked like surgical instruments.

Benches of metal and long metal tables covered with gleaming white enamel or porcelain stood here and there about the room. These were covered with a variety of vats and crucibles, glass and ceramic containers of every size and description. Peering within, she discovered that these vessels held colored fluids and powders of various kinds. Many were marked with labels, but these were lettered in characters unknown to her.

Tall lamps of tubular metal were affixed to wall brackets. Some were illuminated by an unknown power-source, and cast beams of vivid hues upon lumps of protoplasm sealed in closed, transparent vessels. Niamh shuddered and turned her eyes away, for the first time beginning to regret her lack of trepidation in venturing so imprudently into the private domain of her unknown captor.

The lumps of wetly glistening tissue were various organs of the bodies of men and beasts.

And they seemed to be *alive*. . . .

The only exit from the domed room, besides the curtained portal through which she had entered, was a sealed metal door held shut by a system of clamps and levers.

She regarded it dubiously, then attempted to open it. The clamps were not locked, but seemed designed for the purpose of making the inner chamber airtight. She opened the metal door easily and looked within.

A curved wall of spotless white enamel met her eyes. The pungent odor of strong antiseptic assailed her nostrils.

There was nothing in the room but a wax model of a human head fastened in midair to a number of transparent tubes and coppery wires which led to small tanks and engines of curious design.

Puzzled, she entered the inner chamber where the wax model of a human head hung amid these coiling tubes.

The air was clean and fresh and curiously odorless, behind the sharp stench of antiseptic.

The room was brilliantly lit by a sunlike lamp suspended from above.

There was no sound, save for the gurgle of unknown fluids in the tanks, and the drone which arose from the small engines grouped together on the floor beneath the hanging head.

She examined the model curiously.

It was most artistically made, the wax colored with close resemblance to human flesh, and it resembled the head of a young man of her race with a shaved scalp, closed eyes, and loose mouth hanging wetly open.

This object of art, if that is what it was, seemed to her most ghoulish. After inspecting the thing, she turned away with a small, fastidious shudder.

And blundered into a small metal table on wheels which she had not noticed. She stumbled against it, and some of the surgical instruments arranged upon its glistening white upper surface fell to the floor with a clank which seemed loud in the buzzing, gurgling stillness. She froze.

Then the bodiless head opened its eyes and looked at her.

14.

The Sorcerer Quoron

When the bodiless head looked at her, Niamh froze with ghastly horror.

Then she saw that the eyes were wide and unfocused. The gleam of intelligence did not shine in them; they were the blank, unseeing eyes of an idiot-thing.

The loose mouth worked wetly and the head spoke.

Wa-wa-w'-aaah?"

As she stared in horror and revulsion, a dribble of slime drooled from the working lips of the thing as it babbled meaningless noises.

Then a sound came from behind her. A dry cough!

She spun to see a weird, hunched form in the doorway. It was hideous, and curiously disparate. The head was lean, fine-boned, ascetic—even handsome, in a pure, nobly proportioned way.

But its handsomeness ended at the neck.

The body was that of a twisted dwarf with a hunched shoulder and warped, diminutive legs. Swathed in a loose white gown it was, and the gown bulged peculiarly, and in the most surprising places, as if there were portions of the body beneath that gown that bore little or no semblance to the human body.

The creature in the doorway fixed her with a cold, ironic gaze of appraisal. Niamh was very near swooning—the hanging head was still drooling and babbling in

a witless manner behind her—but she drew herself up and
regarded the being who could only be her captor with a
superb pretense of hauteur.

The cold, ironic eyes moved beyond her to the hanging
thing. The slight smile left the thin lips and was replaced
by an expression of sadness mingled with a curious contempt.

"You are a most persistent young woman," observed
the dwarf. "I had thought you safely tucked away, but
here you are, freely wandering my tower and prying into
my most closely guarded secrets. Well, having intruded
upon Wa-Wa's privacy, what do you think of him?"

"Wa-Wa?" she repeated faintly. He nodded at the
thing behind her.

"Yes, I call it that partly because I have to call it
something, and partly because that is the only sound it
seems to know how to make. I have been trying to teach
it human speech, but, alas, in that, as in so much else, my
artistry falls short of its goal. Well, speak up, girl. What
do you think?"

Niamh had recovered some of her self-possession by
now. She had nothing to lose from speaking bluntly, so
she spoke her mind. It did not seem to her that this
hunched, deformed cripple could possibly do her any
harm. Her own body was lithe and strong; if it came to a
contest, she thought it likely she could turn the tables and
make the captor captive.

"I think you should put the pitiful thing out of its
misery," she said coldly. "Why do you permit it to continue in this grisly mockery of life? The humane thing to
do—"

Something flared in the cold, cruel eyes of the dwarf.

"'Mockery of life,' indeed! My dear young woman, you
are looking upon the noblest miracle of science wrought
by human hands on this planet since the dead, forgotten
days of the mighty Kaloodha! Do you dare to think the
thing is only a semblance of life? Gods of The World

Above, woman, *I have removed the head from a living body and kept it alive and functioning for two years!"*

She stared at the cold face of the dwarf, her thoughts unutterable. Now a weird passion flamed in his fathomless gaze and drove vivid color into his sallow cheeks.

"Do you not understand the magnitude of this scientific miracle?" he hissed. "Or are your wits too shallow and mundane to perceive the scope of my discoveries? By a fission so adriot and subtle it were inaccuracy itself to demean it by so crude a term as 'surgery,' I have removed a man's head, sealed the nerve endings, attached the veins and arteries to a sterile pumping system, employed a bellows-like device to replace the lungs, and kept the severed head living and healthy! The hair continues to grow unless shaved . . . the mouth glands salivate as the nostrils inhale the odor of succulent food . . . the eyes respond to light, darkness, and motion . . . the eardrums react to loud sounds . . . *the thing lives, I tell you! Lives!"*

The dwarf's voice rose in a frenzied screech that rang deafeningly through the domed white chamber. The dangling head flinched and began to blubber. Niamh shrank from the dwarf as he limped toward her with a shambling, crablike gait.

Suddenly, the hunched little figure was sinister and even fearsome. His sudden, mercurial transition from cold irony to gibbering fervor took her off-guard.

She perceived that her captor was more dangerous than she had thought at first.

"And its—brain?"

The question fell from her lips in automatic response. It was not a question she had meant to ask, and, looking at the scarlet fury that rose and glared within the dwarf's maniacal gaze, she faltered, and bit her lip, wishing she had not spoken.

Then the frenzy passed. The hunched figure twitched once. The spasm passed; he drooped his head and was, suddenly, somehow pathetic.

"You are right, of course . . . the brain is dead, for all the subtlety of my surgical technique," the dwarf muttered in low tones. "Oh, the sensory nerves respond to stimuli . . . the motor centers still function as if automatically, but—the *mind* is dead; quite dead. For all my science, I cannot help it to think, to reason, to communicate. It is the one goal I have yet to achieve, the one barrier yet unconquered. I can keep the head alive, but the brain dies. . . ."

The dwarf pondered with bowed head for a moment, then raised his eyes upon her again.

"But I shall yet succeed! I believe the problem lies in the oxygen content of the blood. Between the moment when the head is detached from the body and the moment when the veins and arteries are connected to my artificial heart device, the circulation of blood within the brain pauses. During that interval the brain receives no fresh oxygen, which would otherwise have continued to be carried in the fresh blood pumped from the body's heart. The lack of fresh oxygen, although momentary, causes oxygen starvation, and the effect is like that of a stroke." He meditated for a long moment, lost in the intricacies of the problem, plucking at his lower lip with thumb and forefinger; then he said: "Someday—quite soon, I feel—I shall manage to overcome this last remaining obstacle. And then the world shall resound with praise of the arch-scientist, Quoron."

"You mean 'the sorcerer Quoron,' do you not?" Niamh said cuttingly. "For to keep the poor thing in this ghastly state is black sorcery, not science!"

This time her rash, imprudent words did not sting the little cripple to a flare-up of fury. He merely eyed her incuriously, his mind busy with the problem.

"Enough of this idle converse," the dwarf said absently. "Take her back to her cell, Number Nine. I have work to do."

Niamh looked back to the doorway with apprehension.

It was filled now by a huge, lumbering figure, nude, hairless, and immense. Hands the size of a monster's reached for her.

She screamed.

When she recovered from her swoon, Niamh found herself not back in the dry well with its circular walls, but in a comfortably furnished apartment. She was stretched out on a couch draped with colorful silken scarves, and many small soft plump pillows were beneath her.

She jumped to her feet and stared around wildly, wondering if her experiences were driving her mad.

A harsh, well-remembered voice spoke from a concealed aperture.

"Calm yourself, young woman. You have not become deranged, nor are you suffering from delirium."

It was the voice of Quoron.

"Where am I, then? I thought you said—"

"I was originally planning to have Number Nine return you to your former place of captivity," said the sorcerer's voice, "but it occurred to me that, as you had once managed to escape from your former quarters, it would not be wise on my part to encourage you in further unauthorized explorations. Already, your untimely blundering into the sealed chamber has forced me to completely sterilize the air supply and to cleanse all of the objects and surfaces you might have touched with a potent antiseptic. The head must be kept in a completely sterile environment, under controlled conditions, you see. I believe you will find your new accommodations considerably more luxurious than those you previously enjoyed, when first you intruded upon the hospitality of my sanctum ... and also considerably more difficult to escape from."

"Where are you?" Niamh demanded fiercely.

Quoron chuckled. "Quite safely hidden, and watching your every movement from a place of concealment. But do not worry, my dear; I have no intentions of intruding upon your privacy. I will leave you to your own devices now, but be wary. Do not think to elude my hospitality again. Number Nine will have you under constant surveillance, both by night and by day. He has no interest in women, for he has no mind save my will; therefore you may freely undress and bathe under his scrutiny with no less embarrassment than you would at baring your body under the gaze of a pet beast. For Nine is little more than that. Very little more. . . ."

The harsh, ironic voice faded and Niamh felt herself to be alone. She collapsed back upon the silken couch, despair welling up within her.

She was in the clutches of a madman, and helpless to do anything about it.

15.

To Live—Forever!

During her next few days as a prisoner of the sorcerer Quoron in the Opal Tower, Niamh came very close to madness from fear, frustration, and despair.

The apartment in which the dwarf had confined her was in truth comfortable to the point of being luxurious. A warm bath of scented waters was at her disposal, and the apartment contained sanitary facilities superior even to those afforded by her own palace in distant Phaolon. She had a variety of attractive, fresh clothing to wear, and the apartment contained several books and works of art for her amusement.

But a prison is still a prison, no matter if the bars of the cage are made of beautiful gold.

There was no window to the room and the only door, a massive slab of heavy ceramic, was guarded by the unsleeping giant the sorcerer called Number Nine. It was this immense, obscene brute who served her meals, and no matter how intense her appetite might be, the very approach of the monstrosity made her faint with loathing.

Number Nine, she learned from scraps of information gleaned from listening to the rambling discourse of Quoron, was one of a series of surgical experiments—one that had lived.

In an attempt to master the secrets of life and death, and to discover the arcana of Nature herself, Quoron had

"Number Nine, Niamh the Fair, and Quoron."

taken apart human bodies and put them together into new, ghastly hybrids.

Number Nine, for example, had four arms and three legs.

And two heads.

The arms were positioned two to a side, the one above the other. This reorganization of the human body had required the sorcerer to build into the armpit of the first pair sufficient shoulder muscles to render the lower set of arms usuable. In the case of the lower left arm, the grafting of a new musculature had been successful. But the lower right arm dangled limply, pale and wizened, its flaccid open-palmed hand slapping Number Nine's thigh at every step.

The third leg had been built on to an extension of the rear portion of the pelvis, a new hip-socket having been engineered where the coccyx is found on normal bodies. The leg had to be a trifle shorter than the other two, so Quoron had used the right leg of an immature boy for this hind-member.

The body was a walking obscenity. But it was the matter of the twin heads that nauseated the princess the most.

They jutted out from a thickly wattled common neck at sharp angles, and one was a woman's head, and the other was a man's.

Quoron referred to this choice as one of his "little pleasantries."

Both heads were slack-jawed and blank-eyed, and the twin brains were little more than idiots. But the lumbering brute was completely under the control of its master and had utterly no will of its own. Quoron demonstrated this fact one evening by commanding Nine to hold its fingers in a candle-flame until the skin shriveled and popped and crackled like the skin of a sausage on a spit.

Nine whimpered and whined, but did not remove its hand from the white-hot flame until Quoron bade it do so.

That night the dreams of Niamh were horrible. . . .

The sorcerer seldom visited the princess, although he very frequently conversed with his lovely young captive from a place concealed in the walls of the apartment.

These conversations were more in the order of rambling monologues than true conversations, although Niamh at times sought to draw the maniacal dwarf out with questions. Her theory here was, obviously, the more you know about your captor, the more potentially useful information you have at your disposal.

Quoron did not mind being questioned. He loved to talk about his plans for the future, and an intelligent audience was better than a drooling head or a witless, shambling giant.

In this manner Niamh found out the purpose of Quoron's experiments.

They could be summed up in one word: immortality.

The madman could not have enjoyed much of life, confined to a warped and hideous, dwarfed and crippled body. But, it would seem, even life at such a price is more sweetly to be savored than the absence of life.

Quoron had fallen into the same intellectual trap which had already, ages before his time, destroyed the race whose scientific marvels and accomplishments he admired so much—the Kaloodha, the extinct Winged Men who had built the Opal Tower a million years before.

The same madness infected him which had also driven insane the beautiful black supermen of the Flying Cities* which drifted high above the treetops amid the eternal cloud-veil that shields this planet from the piercing emerald rays of its primary.

The lust to live—*forever*.

It was the mad ambition of Quoron to find a way to

---

*   Such as the aerial metropolis of Calidar, which Niamh and her companions previously visited in the third volume of these memoirs, which I edited under the title of *By the Light of the Green Star*.   —*Editor*.

render a human being perpetually invulnerable to the effects of time and change and age.

First he had sought the secret within the body itself, thinking that some gland or organ or nerve center, under the appropriate drugs or stimuli, might immortalize the body and enable it to repair or to replace worn-out tissues. These experiments had led to the creation of such monstrosities as Number Nine.

Failing to find the secret of eternal life in that avenue of research, Quoron had next turned to the preservation of the only essential part of a human body—the brain.

His experiments in this direction had, thus far, resulted in failure.

The bodiless head in the white chamber—the mindless idiot-thing he called, contemptuously, by the name of Wa-Wa—was the only brain he had thus far managed to keep alive for any significant length of time, after removing it from its body.

The brain lived, but the mind was dead.

The problem of continuing the supply of fresh oxygen to the vital brain centers during the difficult process of decapitation was his present area of research.

Quoron now felt that the answer lay in attaching the veins and arteries to the system of valves and pumps he called his artificial heart—*before* the cranium was severed from the torso.

That way the fatal interval would be overcome, during which the mind centers died of oxygen-starvation.

Quoron now felt he was approaching his ultimate goal.

Niamh had never dared inquire of the dwarf his ultimate purpose in holding her captive in the Opal Tower.

She was afraid to, for she feared the worst.

Instead she questioned Quoron as to how he intended to preserve his own life by this method, once he had mastered the technique. After all, one can scarcely decapitate oneself.

He replied that he had foreseen that eventuality. Number Nine would perform the entire operation.

Niamh was incredulous. "That clumsy monstrosity? You would entrust so delicate an operation to—to—?"

"To Number Nine?" He chuckled. "Of course! To whom else could I possibly entrust so excessively difficult a task? The twin brains of Number Nine have been sponged clean of every thought and memory; they are like tablets of fresh clay, ready to be written upon. Once the techniques are perfected, Nine will be schooled with exquisite thoroughness in every step and detail of the process. Why do you think I gave the brute four hands? So that it can perform the operation with twice the speed and twice the care of an ordinary person."

Quoron smiled thinly.

"You need not fear for me, my dear. Nine retains no memory, its dual brain is completely blank. It functions only in obedience to my will, and remembers nothing from one day to another."

But Niamh was not so certain of this.

Sometimes, during the early evening when the candles where lit, as the brute was serving her supper, she observed a strange thing happen.

As the three functional hands were laying the table with deft, mechanical precision, the eyes of the twin heads would stray.

The wavering flame of the candles would catch those dull, mindless eyes. The flames that were identical with the candle-flame in which Quoron had once commanded his pet monster to hold its hands until the skin and flesh of the fingers of that hand crisped and fried.

Was it the flicker of fear Niamh thought she glimpsed in those four dull eyes?

Or was it the memory of pain?

Or was it—just possibly—anger?

The Fourth Book

KARN AMONG THE AMAZONS

16.

The Mind-Search

At length, having failed to discover the whereabouts of Delgan of the Isles, Zorak of Tharkoon, or Niamh the Fair, and having failed as well to find out what had happened to myself, Prince Andar called off the search.

Although he did so with the greatest reluctance, it was obvious to all that further expeditions into the edges of the forest country would be equally as fruitless as those which had already been so tirelessly prosecuted.

The searchers embarked for their return voyage to the royal isle of Komar, leaving behind only Zarqa the Kalood.

The Winged Man politely declined Prince Andar's invitation to return to Komar and rejoin his comrades, the newly married Prince Janchan and Princess Arjala, who were anxiously awaiting news of their lost friends.

I shall remain here in the forest for a time, Zarqa said in the telepathic mode of communication his kind employed in lieu of vocal speech. *It may yet be possible to ascertain the whereabouts of my dear friends. At least, it is my most earnest desire to attempt it.*

"Well, I can certainly understand your determination, Zarqa, and your desire to find your friends," said Andar the Komarian thoughtfully. "But why do you think that you might succeed, where so many of my men have already failed?"

To this query the Winged Man made a polite but largely evasive reply. Always cautious of hurting the feelings of humans, whom he could not help but regard as less fortunate than he, Zarqa restrained himself from giving voice to his real thoughts.

He felt that he, being an immortal, and for that reason less conscious of the passing of time, was capable of far greater patience than were the Komarians. No matter how deeply and sincerely they desired to find and rescue from the perils of the wilderness the strangers who had come to their assistance in reconquering the kingdom of Komar from the Blue Barbarians, they were still mortal, and therefore time-bound. A day, a week, was an appreciable division of time to their way of thinking, because it was a measurable fraction of their lives.

Not so, to Zarqa the Kalood. To search the worldwide forest of gigantic trees for a year or even ten, meant nothing to a being whose lifespan was to be measured in many millions of years. Zarqa was more than willing to devote so long a time to the search. Not only did the Kalood suffer less than did humans from deprivation, due to his enormously tough and resilient physical makeup, but he seldom required nutriment and never needed to sleep.

And I, Karn, was the first true friend he had found in all the world since the death of the last of his kind a million years ago. I had been the first human to extend to Zarqa the warm handclasp of friendship and, in so doing, to bridge the abyss which lay between his kind and my own.

Zarqa was unable to forget that. He was ready to devote the remainder of his life, however long his immortality might last, to the search for me and my friends, or for our remains.

Moreover, it was undeniably true that Zarqa possessed one unique faculty which made his ability to search the forest of mile-high trees far more swiftly and easily than could Andar's men, for all their numbers. And that was his wings.

Therefore, bidding Prince Andar and the others farewell for a time, Zarqa watched as they embarked for the voyage back to Komar. Then he turned, spread his great batlike golden wings, and glided from the branch into the green-gold twilight world of the giant trees.

The immediate edge of the world-forest had already been thoroughly combed by the Komarian force. They had started at the approximate point at which the sky craft, bearing Delgan and Zorak and Niamh, had been observed to enter the vast wall of tree-trunks, and had searched with minute care along the edge and then deeper into the almost impenetrable woods.

Zarqa, therefore, wasted no energy in retracing their steps but sailed deeper yet into the forest, and then began to scrutinize the great trees, bough by bough, branch by branch, for any sign of human habitation.

With his enormous patience and his lack of any need for rest or sleep or food, the gaunt Kalood was able to search tirelessly, even into the hours of darkness; for his visual organs, designed along somewhat different lines than those of the human eye, required far less light in order to see.

Before leaving the royal isle of Komar, Zarqa had imbibed of the golden mead which was all the nutriment his physical system required. He could now go for many weeks, even for months, before he would begin to suffer from any lack of sustenance. When the extinct Kaloodhan race, with their miraculous super-science, had redesigned their bodies more than two thousand millennia before, they had wisely eliminated many of the built-in limiting factors which impaired the efficiency of their anatomy. They had done the job well. . . .

After some days of tireless and unceasing search, Zarqa came to realize that his present mode of investigation was likely to prove ultimately unprofitable.

It became obvious to the Winged Man that since they had first entered into the vast and towering forest, his friends had traveled or wandered or had been transported far away from their point of entry. He had, of course, no knowledge of the various mishaps and adventures which had befallen his former comrades, but they were simply nowhere to be found.

They were, quite obviously, still traveling. He reasoned that every hour and every day which he continued to waste by searching in his present slow, meticulous fashion, they were doubtless still voyaging far afield.

Before long, Zarqa thought of a more efficient mode of searching, a method by which he might cover enormous territory much faster, yet search just as carefully and minutely as before.

The solution to his problem was to search by mind alone.

When Nature denied the Winged Men the power of articulate speech, she repaired that omission by bequeathing to them the ability to communicate on a purely telepathic level. To the Kaloodha, then, it naturally follows, the mental radiations of a mind are as distinctly individual as personal speech is to us. Whereas we recognize differences in tone and pitch and timbre as characteristics of the individual, and recognize our friends' voices even when unable to see them, so it is with the telepathically sensitive Kaloodha such as Zarqa.

I do not know precisely how the Winged Men identify individual mental radiations—whether it is by differences in the wavelength of thought waves or from the uniquely different configurations of each mental wavefront—but, however the manner in which they accomplish the feat, it is demonstrably possible for a Kalood to pick out the radiations of a single mind with which it is familiar, among many thousands.

So Zarqa began the mind-search.

Once before he had searched in this manner. That was

when he and his companions had become separated by
night during their flight from the Flying City of Calidar.
Then he had searched for the mind of Ralidux the Black
Immortal, but he could as easily have striven to locate Niamh the Fair or even the Goddess Arjala, for with their
minds he had become by that time familiar.*

Since Zarqa had no way of guessing which of his lost
comrades he would encounter first, the Winged Man held
firmly in mind the "flavor" and "style" and "color" of the
mind radiations of Niamh and Delgan and Karn simultaneously. Only the mind of Zorak was not sufficiently
known to him to afford Zarqa the chance to hold his mental characteristics firmly in memory during the search.
These curious terms, by the way, are the closest that the
Kalood can come in translating into human terminology
the distinctly differing characteristics of individual human
minds to which he is sensitive.

Now, mental radiations are not limited to line-of-sight.
Neither are they blocked or dispersed or deflected by solid
barriers, such as the boles or branches of the great trees
of the forest (indeed, according to Zarqa, most solids are
completely transparent to thought waves). Therefore,
using the mind alone to search, the Winged Man was able
to cover immense tracts of territory in very little time.

For another full day he flew without resting, ranging
the forest in an ever-expanding spiral, his mental sensors
alert and keen. The dim pulsations of brute mentalities he
detected, and the keener, more articulated radiations of
the minds of a variety of human brains. But nowhere did
he catch the slightest trace or whisper of the three minds
he sought.

Until night had fallen, that is.

* The incident to which the author refers at this point in his
narrative is described in the fourth volume of this history, a
book to which I have given the title *As the Green Star Rises*.
—*Editor*.

Then, quite suddenly, there came to his alert concentration the distant echo of a familiar mind.

As soon as he was able to discern with some nicety the distance and direction of that mental source, he homed in on it. Flying on swift and tireless vans, the wise Kalood approached the position of the mind which was a familiar one.

It was in a peculiar set of surroundings, and more than a little danger compassed it around. But Zarqa arrowed through the dark night to come to the aid of one of the minds for which he had so untiringly searched ... and found himself amid a frozen tableau of astonishing terror.

17.

A Chance Discovery

During my first few days as a captive of the band of wild girls, I had sufficient opportunity to observe and even to experience their dislike of all males.

The girls kept me busy at the most menial and degrading of tasks, and seized upon every excuse to heap abuse and mistreatment upon me. I was forced to go continually naked, and my appearance afforded my savage captresses endless amusement. They also enjoyed seeing me toil for them, and I was beaten with a switch for every conceivable infraction of the rules governing my behavior.

At nights I slept on a crude pallet in a rough lean-to that adjoined the cabin in which the chieftainess of my tormentors dwelt. I refer, of course, to Varda.

My sleeping quarters were crudely built and of flimsy construction. On frequent occasions, it occurred to me that when and if the opportunity to make a break for freedom ever came, I should have little if any difficulty in getting out. Unfortunately, however, the savage band was ever on the alert to the possibility of my escape, and took every precaution to prevent it.

When, during the day, I was sent out to gather fruits or nuts or berries, a group of the littler savages accompanied me, and I performed these labors with a choke halter about my throat. To this was affixed a tether which the girls either held and cruelly jerked upon, or which was

tied securely to a twig or some other relatively solid pro-
tuberance.

Very frequently, my wrists or ankles were tied together
with bonds which, while they did not completely render
me immobile, served at least to hamper and to restrict my
freedom of movement. When I was permitted to sleep, my
wrist or leg was bound securely to an iron ring sunk into
the branch upon which the house of Varda was built.

My bonds, by the way, were neither ropes nor lengths
of woven material, but strips of tough, well-seasoned
rawhide. While I still retained a physical strength and a
vitality which was considerably superior to that of a
normal boy of my age and weight and height—a lingering
aftereffect of the magical Elixir of Light of which I had
imbibed long ago at the command of Sarchimus the
Wise—it requires more than sheer brute force to sever so
tenacious a form of bondage as rawhide. Nothing less
than a sharp knife-blade would do the trick. I watched
continuously for the chance to steal a knife or some similar sharp-edged tool, but the opportunity never once
presented itself.

It began to look as if my plans for escape were
hopeless pipe dreams. . . .

While the girls beat me and used me with the utmost
humiliation and scorn, mistreating me in every manner
which their agile and vindictive wits could devise, they
neither starved me nor managed to break my spirit.

I remained aloof and unperturbed, absorbing their cru-
elest punishments with a somber and uncomplaining mien.
For this example of stoicism, I ask no particular credit,
neither do I regard my behavior under these adverse
conditions to be particularly praiseworthy or exemplary. I
lived in the constant hope and expectation of freedom,
which might come at any moment and in the most unexpected manner.

To be frank, I expected to be rescued, for I knew that
my absence from Komar would not long go unnoticed,

and that when both the sky-sled and myself were discovered to be missing, my friends would swiftly put two and two together, and arrive at the appropriate sum. Nor would they waste time in coming after me.

That they might have unexpected difficulties in finding me, I did not at that time envision. I had, you will understand, by this time so thoroughly become lost and disoriented, that I had not the slightest idea of quite how far I had strayed from the point at which I had first entered the forest, nor of quite how deeply my wanderings had taken me into the depths of the wilderness of gigantic trees. That forest, of course, stretched in an unbroken mass from horizon to horizon and from pole to pole, covering, insofar as any of us then knew, the entire surface of the World of the Green Star. The only portion of the planet's surface which was definitely known to be free and unencumbered by the world-forest, was, of course, that section occupied by the Komarian Sea.

So, as you will understand, I had plenty of room to be lost in!

Remaining in my blissful state of ignorance, and expecting at any moment the arrival of my friends to extricate me from my present plight and predicament, I worried little over the future and endured, with that stoicism and fortitude I have already described, the cruel treatment I suffered at the hands of these spiteful and malicious children.

Nor did I hate my savage captors.

But these expectations, of course, did not prohibit me from keeping a close and careful watch out for a chance to escape on my own. Confident are those who help themselves.

In all, I must admit that my personal feelings toward my savage little captors were of a somewhat ambivalent nature. I could not quite find it within me to despise them, for all the abuse and discomfiture I endured at their hands.

At a young and tender age they had been wantonly savaged by the slavers who had carried them off forcibly into the wilderness, and by that act had seemingly doomed them to lives of hopeless despair. That they had managed to escape from the hands of the marauders had in no way alleviated the precarious and perilous situation into which they had been thrust.

Nor could they be blamed for their fear and loathing and mistrust of my sex, for it was at the hands of men like myself that they had suffered untold horrors and humiliations, from which indignities only the chance attack of the swarm of *zzumalaks,* or giant killer-bees, had delivered them.

Helpless to find their way home again, the girls had simply ventured out into the wilderness, at length finding the safe, secure nook in which they had built their camp and made it their home. Many of the tools and weapons which had formerly been the possessions of the slavers they had carried off with them, for to the survivor belongs the possessions of the slain.

The only other thing they had borne away from their dire experience at the mercy of the slave-marauders was their vicious and virulent hatred, loathing, and mistrust of all things male and masculine.

Which was only natural and human, and, certainly, quite understandable.

But which was, from my point of view, regrettable; for that hatred unfortunately included myself.

My chances for escape were very soon to take on healthy and renewed vigor. Here is how it came about.

One day my giggling captors led me farther down the great branch on which their encampment was constructed than until now I had been permitted to travel.

The reason for this lay in the discovery of an unexpected colony of the giant tree-snails, or *huoma,* whose tender and delicious meat made a succulent and desirable treat to our appetites. In general we lived on more spartan and even vegetarian fare.

Under the watchful eye of the girls I pried the huge snails one by one from their positions, and bundled them into nets. Later, back at the camp, we would unshell the creatures and boil them in their own juices.

Quite a considerable number of the huge, thick-witted, slow-moving, gentle, and quite harmless monster snails had for some reason gathered on the branch, so the work occupied us for the remainder of that day.

The last few snails had sluggishly sought to avoid capture by crawling, in their lumbering form of perambulation, around to the underside of the branch.

In order to gather these last, reluctant survivors of the snail colony, I had to venture the risky business of climbing around beneath the branch. The situation was precarious and not without a certain element of danger, for I was suspended by ropes held in the hands of my careless and capricious mistresses, who threatened to let me fall if I did not quickly accomplish my tasks.

The job was difficult, and tiring, but for a very good reason I was delighted that it had fallen to my lot.

This peculiar contradiction lay in the fact of what I discovered from my upside-down position at the end of the rope.

The sky-sled was tethered to a down-jutting twig.

Evidently the girls had, with time, become curious as to the nature of the odd contrivance in which I had been curled up asleep when they found me and made me their captive.

A second expedition had retraced the path taken by the first, and, when the utter weightlessness of the vehicle was discovered (which made it easy to bear the prize home to the girls' camp), they had retrieved the peculiar treasure and it now reposed, safely tethered, at no very great distance from the tree-houses.

If I could somehow manage to contrive my escape—the means of flight to freedom was close at hand.

The tantalizing presence of the sky-sled drove new life into my hopes for escape.

That night, as you can easily imagine, I tossed and turned, schemes tumbling through my feverish brain, and got very little sleep.

18.

Varda

The nearness of the sky-sled put escape virtually within my grasp. But it did nothing to make escape a reality. For still was I bound and watched and tethered every moment of the day and night.

So, for the time being, I held my peace and waited things out, ever alert for the slightest slip or inattention on the part of the wild girls when I might seize opportunity by the forelock.

And still my friends did not come.

The ever-present rivalry between Varda and Iona filled the air with the tension of an unresolved conflict. Iona was continually challenging the authority of Varda, the wisdom of her decisions, and the justice of her rules. Moreover, she was constantly complaining, quarreling, criticizing. Varda kept her temper, for the most part, although I for one cannot understand how she managed to accomplish this.

But she was fully aware of the fact that Iona hated and envied her, and desired more than anything else to supplant her in the chieftaincy of the Amazon band. She knew all too well that the jealous older girl was whispering and scheming behind her back, but there was little she could do about it.

Instead, she took her frustrations and tensions out on me.

I was the butt of her fury and the object of her derision. Nothing I did pleased her sufficiently, and in no way could I satisfy her demands of perfection. I was punished, sometimes by scorn and mockery and public humiliation, but very often by punishment of a more corporeal nature.

Through it all I held my tongue, maintained my dignity as best I could, and watched and waited for the chance to make a break for freedom. Would it never come? Would I never be free of these malicious girls, free to seek my own lost beloved amid the trackless forest? Even now she might be dead, or dying, or suffering unendurable torments or privations, or in deadly danger.

It was the unknown fate of Niamh the Fair that was my saddest torment; and my love for her proved a steadfast anchor to which I clung, no matter how furious the gales which swept about me and sought to drag me down into the depths of despair. Silently, within my secret heart, I vowed a thousand times to win my way to her side—somehow, somehow!—though all the world stood ranked against me.

Very gradually there came a change in the manner with which Varda regarded me. It was neither a change for the better, or a change which I liked.

Sometimes, as I knelt scrubbing the floor, or bent over the kitchen utensils to cleanse them, or gathered firewood for the hearth, I was conscious of her eyes lingering upon my naked manhood in a curious manner. It roused within me a tingling apprehension which I can neither quite describe nor account for.

It happened the first time one morning while I was cutting wood for the cookfire.

The girl outlaws had carried off an axelike tool from the camp of the slave-marauders, and with this I was busily engaged in splitting the great slabs of bark from the branch upon which the camp was built, cutting these slabs into slender lathes, and bundling them with twine for the hearth.

The morning was hot and humid, the air windless. Leaves, which were bent awry in such a manner as to screen the huts and cabins from aerial view, hung motionless in the steamy air.

I had been at work for about an hour and my naked hide glistened with perspiration, which ran in long wet rivulets down my belly and thighs, cutting paths through the bark-dust. The daylight gleamed in highlights along the raised ridges of the muscles of my legs, and the great thews which swelled along my back and shoulders. Each time I drew erect and lifted the heavy ax above my head, my powerfully developed pectoral muscles stood forth in sharp relief, and the corded muscles of my taut midsection grew rock-ribbed and hard.

I became aware of Varda's gaze upon my nakedness.

The expression on her face was unreadable. Her eyes were bright and hot, yet somehow dreamy as well. Her gaze lingered on the musculature of my chest and arms, which by now were deeply bronzed from many weeks of exposure to the rays of the Green Star, during the time I had been marooned with Shann on the desert island amid the Sea of Komar.

The thirteen-year-old girl stood, her body turned a little from me, one slim hand at her throat, her head twisted to observe my body. I saw that her shallow adolescent breasts rose and fell with the rapidity of her breathing, and that high color rose to mantle her cheeks.

Catching my inquiring gaze, her eyes widened and fell, veiled behind heavy lashes, and she turned away.

But not before I saw the burning color of her cheeks.

A day or two later, while setting the long table for the evening meal, she had cause to reprimand me for a fancied clumsiness. She slapped and scratched me as I stood unresisting, my arms folded upon my chest, my head lowered. Suddenly, her blows softened almost to so many caresses. She drew the fingers of one hand, slowly, down the bulge of my biceps while her other hand went out, tentatively, to touch my bent back.

I heard her catch her breath.

The moment was electric with excitement. I said nothing, did nothing. Her hand removed itself, and the next thing I knew, she had left the cabin, and did not return for hours, not even to join in the evening meal.

She did not return, in fact, until after the fall of darkness. As I lay unsleeping in my cubicle, tethered to the metal ring, I heard her come slamming in, then the creak of her cot as she flung her restless body upon it. Then, a bit later, I heard the muffled sound of her weeping.

She cried herself to sleep that night. But I . . . I did not sleep at all, but lay staring up into the darkness, thinking my own thoughts.

Many times during the days and nights thereafter I felt the sensitive pressure of her gaze upon my body as I toiled at my tasks. It seemed to me that Varda sought every pretense she could think of to be in my proximity, and that she found many a reason to touch me or to stand very close to me.

I pretended to notice nothing, hoping I was mistaken about the cause of her curious malady, and its nature. For it was not really either rare or curious, the fever which, as I suspected, had Varda in its grip.

It was a sickness as old as the very world.

The affection which Varda evidently felt for me had an adverse effect on our relationship. Instead of being kinder and more gentle in her treatment, she flew more frequently into wild and furious rages, during which she scratched and pummeled me unmercifully. She fell into black moods of brooding, or into sulky passions during which nothing could rouse her or lighten her mood.

When she had cause to punish me, she did so with the

utmost cruelty and vigor. It was almost as if, in punishing me, she was somehow inflicting punishment upon herself.

Although I am no psychologist, and, no more than any other man, pretend to have anything but the slightest and most cursory understanding of women, I believe I came to an understanding of her dilemma. It was the conflict between her private emotions and her public position.

The savage girls had been misused and outraged by their brutal captors. Slaying the marauders who had enslaved them had not sufficed to revenge them fully upon the male sex. So they maintained a virulent hatred of the other half of the human species, and, as I was the only male around, took this out on me.

So—while all that was womanly in the heart of the teen-aged girl was beginning to respond to my own maleness—this was in conflict with Varda's own ingrained loathing of the masculine gender. She loathed and hated herself, on some deep, hidden layer of her being, for looking upon me with the dawning of desire.

Being only human, she punished me for the mere fact that I was a male, and that she found my maleness arousing.

The situation was potentially an explosive one.

I literally held my breath and stayed out of her way as best I could. It goes without saying that, neither by look, word, act, nor gesture, did I encourage her interest in me or display any awareness or response to her own youthful and violent passion.

This, however, seemed only to heap fuel on the flames that raged within the girl.

It was a horrible situation to be in. I could see the danger of it, but I knew myself to be completely helpless to avert the catastrophe I could so clearly foresee.

There is nothing more ghastly than the position of the prophet who, although forewarned, can do nothing to avoid the impending doom he senses.

19.

The Eavesdropper

The increasing interest paid to me by Varda became more and more obvious, until it reached the point at which I was surprised that none of the other girls in the savage little band noticed it.

The peculiar expression that appeared in her eyes whenever the teen-aged girl looked into my face disturbed me profoundly. It was eloquent, if unspoken—a dare, almost a challenge. But a challenge to which I did not dare give any response. In fact, I ignored her as much as was possible, under the circumstances, and pretended to be oblivious of the way in which she virtually flaunted her half-naked young body before me at every opportunity.

The situation was drawing toward a climax, I knew; and yet I was helpless to do anything to avoid the explosion I foresaw so clearly.

Again and again, over the next day or two, I wished most vehemently that my friends would come to rescue me from this explosive tinderbox of emotions.

But they did not come. . . .

One evening matters came to a head, and the manner of it was as follows:

The girls had, after considerable tinkering, managed to figure out how to open the storage compartment which was located in the tail of the sky-sled. I am only deducing this from available evidence, but there was indeed a lag of some days between the time I discovered the wild girls had salvaged my abandoned aerial vehicle, and the time they found the supplies and gear I had stored in the storage compartment.

It would have been a simple matter, had they but directed me to open the tail storage compartment for them, of course, but they gave me no such orders. I presume it was but another example of their fierce bias against my sex: to have instructed me to open the compartment for them would have been to admit openly that they did not know how the lock worked. This admission, I suppose, would have damaged their imagined superiority over all males. So they had to work it out for themselves.

When they did so, the girls had a holiday with my stores and provisions.

Before leaving the royal isle of Komar I had, you will remember, stocked my vehicle with meats, jellies, fruit, and pastry, and the peculiar purple cheeselike concoction which the Komarians regard as a rare delicacy.

These were not exactly the most ideal provisions imaginable for a journey, but were all that I had ready access to in my hurry to be off following the trail of Niamh, Zorak, and Delgan. I had, quite simply, plundered the foodstuffs from the leftovers that remained after the wedding-feast of Prince Janchan and the Goddess Arjala.

Since the savage girls subsisted largely on the fruits and nuts and berries of the forest, leavened out with occasional *huoma* meat, this festive fare from the banquet tables of Komar was a welcome treat to them. That evening they made a feast in the largest of the huts.

If you recall my description of the events leading up to my hasty departure from the island of the Komarians, you will also remember that, in lieu of any other drinkables, I stocked the sky-sled with several bottles of the effervescent golden wine of Komar.

This delicacy, in particular, delighted the palate of the

little savages . . . and led to the crisis I had so long foreseen, while remaining powerless to circumvent.

The girls got drunk!

The only fluids they had imbibed in recent months had
been rainwater and dew, collected from the curled upper
surfaces of the enormous leaves that sheltered their encampment from any chance observation. The water was
pure and clear and drinkable enough, to be sure, but
somewhat lacking in flavor.

The golden wine of Komar, however, was quite another
matter.

As they drank deep of the potent beverage, their faces
grew flushed, their eyes began to sparkle, their behavior
became raucous, and a mood of hilarity dominated the
festive board.

In particular, it was their thirteen-year-old leader,
Varda, who drank most deeply of the intoxicant. Her
color deepened under the influence of the delicious wine,
her eyes became humid, her movements languid yet tense,
feverish, and sensual.

One by one the little girls wearied of singing and frol-
icking and squabbling. The wine had gone directly to
their heads, which was not surprising, since in all likeli-
hood it was the first strong drink they had enjoyed in the
three quarters of a year or more since they had managed
to escape from the slaver's camp.

It occurred to me that I might very possibly turn this
event to my own advantage. That is, if the savage girls got
drunk enough they might sleep so soundly that I could
break free without being discovered. Then all I had to do
was find my way back to the sky-sled and fly away to
freedom.

It was certainly worth a try.

However, the wine had a somewhat different effect on
my girl captors than the one I had hoped for.

One by one, the littler girls became woozy, then sleepy

and went off to their sleeping-furs. Eventually I was left alone with Varda.

The wine she had imbibed heightened the color in her cheeks and put a vivacious sparkle in her eyes. It also heated her blood.

"Come here, slave," she snarled, tugging at my leash. She brought me over to where she sat, or rather sprawled, and forced me to my knees before her. Then she looked me over carefully, thoughtfully, a feverish glitter in her eyes that I did not like.

"For a man-cub, you're not at all bad-looking," the girl said hoarsely. She licked her lips, glancing about almost guiltily, as if to make certain we were unobserved.

I said nothing.

Then she bent forward suddenly, seized a handful of my yellow hair, tugged my head back, and kissed me. When I resolutely failed to respond to her kiss, she wrapped her arms about my neck and kissed me again, this time more deeply.

She broke off the kiss, gasping, to peer around, again as if half fearful we were being observed.

I did not like the languid glow in her eye, nor the way she moistened her lips with the small pointed tip of her soft pink tongue.

I opened my mouth, about to protest, but before I could say a word the girl abandoned all pretense and flung herself upon me, covering my face and throat with hot, panting kisses. Her warm, lithe, body pressed against me in a frenzy, and her feverish, trembling caresses were curiously intermingled with sobbing endearments.

She behaved as if possessed. As I failed to respond, and strove to maintain a clear head, remaining adamant to her entreaties, her trembling caresses turned into slaps and blows. Sobbing wildly, tearful eyes gleaming through her disordered tresses, she scratched me like a wildcat and pummeled me unmercifully.

Finally, she collapsed against me, weeping as if her childish heart were broken.

I had striven with all the fortitude within me to avoid responding to her warm and wild caresses, turning my thoughts to Niamh my beloved, and ignoring her entreaties as I ignored her curses. Throughout this humiliating ordeal, then, I had managed, however barely, to remain aloof and unaroused, although I must confess my hot young blood raged within me. The girl was savagely exciting in her disheveled, animal passion. But my heart belonged to another, and I resisted her seductive enticements with might and main.

And then it was that I saw the face at the window.

For the purposes of ventilation, square openings had been cut in the bark-slab walls of Varda's cabin, and sections of dead yellow leaves hung over these, propped open by lengths of twig to permit the circulation of air.

The white face that peered in at us from the square of blackness had evidently observed us for some time. It was pale, wide-eyed, distraught. Scorn and cold fury and the awful gleam of vengeance was visible in the green eyes, and the mouth was curled in a fierce, gloating smile of vindictive triumph.

Only for a moment did the face hang there before it vanished. But in that moment the shock of finding ourselves observed made me stiffen my body, and when I did so, Varda, whose arms were clasped about my neck, raised her head and looked at the window.

She gasped in horror—for the face at the window had been the face of Iona.

20.

The Moment of Truth

Varda gasped and sprang to her feet, staring wild-eyed at the window. But the white, scornful face of Iona was no longer there. The girl ran over to the door, ripped it open, and stared out into the night. There was no sign of the eavesdropper to be seen, apparently.

Varda returned listlessly to the cabin and sagged wearily against the table. Her face was drained, empty.

"I think she saw us," she whispered faintly.

"I know she did," I said.

The girl's temper flared. She turned on me, spitting viciously. "If only you had never come among us, with your vile maleness—!" she hissed, her eyes murderous.

"I did not come of my own free will," I said reasonably. "You forced me at spear-point." The truth of this seemed to exhaust her spiteful temper. She nodded dully, saying nothing. Then she began to whimper; she was, after all, little more than a child.

It suddenly occurred to me how I might turn this disastrous misfortune to my own advantage.

"What will Iona do now?" I asked urgently. The girl shrugged.

"She will tell the rest of the girls that I broke our rule against men," she said listlessly. "Against—you know—having to do with men. They will . . ."

"Give the chieftainship to Iona?" I asked sharply. "Depose you? Outlaw you—force you out into the forest alone?"

She nodded slowly. "Perhaps even ... kill me. I don't know!" Then she whirled on me again, her eyes narrowing and filled with venom. In this temper she was very dangerous, I knew.

"And it's all *your* fault," she snapped.

"Then let me make reparations," I urged her. "Let me save you from this danger. Cut me free—the knife, there, at your belt! Let us escape together. My sky-sled—the flying vehicle in which I came here—is tethered not very far up the branch. Only I know how to operate it. It can fly us away from here swifter even than if we rode a great *zaiph*. Together we can be safe, and I will protect you against the dangers of the wild."

These words came out of me in a breathless rush, and she blinked thoughtfully, absorbing this new idea. Her hand strayed to her belt, that bit of rawhide which held the skins about her slender body, and the tips of her fingers toyed absently with the handle of her knife.

She hesitated, glancing back at the doorway which stood open and was filled with empty darkness. The girl bit her lips uncertainly, trying to think what to do. As if I were another telepath like Zarqa, I could read the thoughts which seethed through her troubled mind:

Perhaps it would be better if I slid this knife between his ribs, rather than flee into the unknown alone with only a brutal male to dominate and abuse me. . . . Then, when Iona comes with the girls, I could lie and say he forced himself upon me and that I was only struggling to free myself from his embrace. . . . No one would ever be able to prove the truth. . . . I could say that Iona lied. Everyone knows how jealous she is of me, and how she twists the truth to make me look bad. . . .

Then she turned, as if reaching a decision, and looked me straight in the eyes.

"If I run away with you, will you become my lover?"

she asked. The knife-blade was naked and ready in her hand.

The moment of truth had come at last.

"No," I said. The light that flashed up in her eyes was not pleasant to see.

Flushed with triumph, Iona scampered agilely down the rungs of the ladder which led to the lower huts where the littler girls of the band slept in dormitory style. The voluptuous teen-ager was aglow with delighted gloating. *At last,* she thought, *that bossy little hussy has played directly into my hands!*

Iona threw back her head in a grimace of triumph that made her lovely face momentarily ugly. Her wild peal of laughter rang loud in the humid stillness of the night.

All around her, the world-forest was drenched in utter gloom. The moonless nights of Lao are abysses of unbroken blackness, and the inhabitants of the forest world are unaccustomed to venture abroad during the hours of darkness, except on furtive missions of stealth and secrecy.

Iona was, for this reason, alone in the night. The wild band of Amazon girls were not used even to the posting of sentinels during the night hours, there being no particular reason to do so.

The night was as black as the bitterness in Iona's heart, and as bottomless as the depth of rancor within that heart. Long, long had she seethed inwardly with jealousy and envy of the pert tomboy who had assumed command of the savage little band. Longer still had Iona dreamed hungrily of somehow seizing the position of dominance which, in her mind, the younger girl had far too long enjoyed.

At last the fulfillment of her dreams was within her grasp.

The girl again permitted that grimace of triumph to

play gloatingly across her features, in an expression that was half smile, half snarl. She felt glorious, superb!

"How could I not have guessed that the man-cub would tempt her to betray herself," the girl panted with a wild, shaky laugh. "She likes men after all. How she must have enjoyed the way the slavers handled her! She lied all the while, saying we did not need males, and that she loathed them, and would kill more if she could! And then—to kiss and caress a skinny, half-grown forest boy! *Ahh!* The liar!"

It was not easy to make one's way down the ladder rungs in the dark, for the pitch was precarious, and some of the twig sections nailed to the branch were wobbly and insecure. More than once, Iona slipped and almost fell.

Finally, she reached the big cabin where several of the little girls she had particularly tried to enlist in her following slept. She paused on the porch for a moment to calm her thudding heart and to catch her breath. Then she un-latched the catch and threw the door open and strode in-side to rouse the sleeping children.

It did not take Iona long to awake the sleepy, befud-dled, half-intoxicated girls from their slumbers, nor to breathlessly spew forth the story of that intimate scene which she had spied upon through the open window, nor to sting the little savages to anger with her malicious in-terpretation of what she had seen.

The hatred and loathing of everything male had been with the forest girls so long that it seemed natural and normal to their way of thinking: a universal law that preached the male of the species was vile and cruel and nasty, and the female pure and noble. By this time, the younger girls quite believed in this perverted gospel, and, in all fairness, the abuse and mistreatment they had en-dured at the hands of the brutal band of slave-marauders who had torn them from their homes, and used them as they pleased, did much to ratify their bias against all men.

Now, to learn that Varda, their leader, their lawmaker,

the older girl they all idolized and admired, had betrayed this most vital and sacred doctrine by fondling and cuddling with the captive boy-slave seemed to them an outrage too vile to be endured.

They came boiling out of their cabin in a fury, like a swarm of *zzumalak* whose nesting place has been violated.

Shrieking, the girls swarmed up the ladder rungs to the branch above, rousing some of the older girls who slept alone or in pairs in the smaller huts. Before long the entire band of little savages was clamoring at the door to the house of their leader.

Iona shouldered her way through the yelling mob, her face glowing with the emotion which gripped her heart, her eyes flashing with triumph.

Signaling for silence with an imperious gesture, she flung the door wide.

The savage girls peered in, to confront a surprising sight ... a sight they had not expected to see ... and a sight at which the heart of Iona froze in terrible consternation.

The Fifth Book

SWORDS AGAINST PHAOLON

21.

On the March

Now it is perhaps time that we returned to consider what has happened to Zorak the Bowman. When we last saw the stalwart captain of Tharkoon, he had been rendered captive by the scarlet horde, a gigantic army of warrior ants, under the despotic rule of Rkhith. And, it should be added, of that wily and cunning arch-villain, Delgan, formerly Warlord of the ·Blue Barbarians, now counselor-in-chief to the insect monarch.

The ant-army advanced through nightly forays until at length it was in the vicinity of Niamh's own realm, Phaolon, the Jewel City. Zorak assumed, probably with some accuracy, that it was Delgan's own scheme to assault the city of Karn's beloved princess. The mighty bowman of Tharkoon by now had begun to realize the tenacity of Delgan's nature; once your enemy, he was your foe forever. If he could not destroy Karn and Niamh himself, he could at least conspire to overthrow their city and butcher its inhabitants.

During the period of his imprisonment by the *kraan*, it had so chanced that Zorak had enjoyed no occasion to converse privately with his former comrade, the great ant, Xikchaka. But as the last day of the march on Phaolon drew near, Xargo, the forger-of-weapons, who had been put in charge of Zorak by the ant-king, had cause to dispatch the bowman on an errand. This errand, as it happened, took the Tharkoonian near the squadron commanded by Xikchaka.

Thus the two met again, for the first time since Xikchaka had betrayed the human into the hands of his fellow ants, after Zorak had helped the ant warrior to escape from the cannibal blossom, and tended his needs when Xikchaka was too feeble to tend to himself.

The two confronted each other. Zorak drew himself up to his full height, crossing his massive arms upon his broad chest, and regarding the monster insect with a level, expressionless look.

The warrior ant returned his gaze. Since his head was armored in tough scarlet chitin, the features of Xikchaka were incapable of any display of emotion or alteration of expression, and the glitter of his ink-black eyes was similarly devoid of any sign of feeling or remorse.

"Greetings, Zorak," he hailed the human warrior in his buzzing, clicking, rasping imitation of man-speech. "How has Zorak adjusted to his new condition in life? Has he been mistreated at the mandibles of Xikchaka's kind?"

"I return your greetings, Xikchaka," replied the bowman in a calm, dignified tone. "Xikchaka will perhaps be gratified to hear that Zorak has been treated well, and is comfortable in all ways, save one alone."

"And what is that?" inquired the insect-creature solemnly.

"I am not free," said Zorak. The warrior ant regarded him in silence for a time.

Then: "What is 'free'?"

Zorak could not restrain the slight smile which touched his grim lips. It was, after all, a question which might give pause to the most learned of philosophers.

"To be free is to be one's own master," he said feelingly. "To come and go at one's will, and as one wishes, without the permission of any other individual. This is the one quality of life which Zorak lacks. And, lacking it, all other things have lost their savor and are meaningless."

The giant *kraan* considered this for a time, his knobbed antennae jerking and twitching.

"Is one ever truly free, whether *kraan* or human?" the emotionless creature questioned in return.

"Some of us are freer than others, at any rate," said Zorak stoutly. "In the wilderness we were free, you and I."

"Free, yes—to starve, to perish from thirst, to fall beneath the rending fangs of the first predator which came upon us," commented Xikchaka. "In the horde, all of the difficulties of life are made simple; all decisions are made for us, all wishes are anticipated and answered before they can be articulated. There is no question of what to do or how to do it: one but follows the directions given by one's superior. Surely, Zorak will admit that one is more comfortable when there are no decisions to be made, no problems to be solved, and when one has only to follow orders."

"More comfortable, perhaps; but not more healthy. For to rely upon another for instruction in every act is to starve and stifle the initiative, to blunt and sap the will, and to reduce all of one's faculties. Suppose Xikchaka more clearly perceives the necessities of the moment than does his nominal superior? Suppose Xikchaka has yearnings, aspirations, and intellectual interests for which his superior has neither understanding nor patience. Will not, then, the heart of Xikchaka go unsatisfied? If he has but no other purpose in life than to obey instructions, he limits himself to a role which is purely mechanical. It is no wonder to Zorak that Xikchaka's kind have lost or submerged the gentler and more humane emotions—love, kindness, mercy, and that very noble and precious quality we term 'friendship.' When one ceases to be personally responsible for the outcome of one's actions, one becomes an emotionless robot. In Zorak's society, each individual bears innumerable responsibilities toward one's family and friends. A kindness must be repaid with a kindness, or the balance of civilized society turns to either indifference or selfishness."

Xikchaka absorbed this, his antennae twitching as if in agitation of mind. Finally he spoke, and when he did the words came slowly.

"To accept personal responsibility for all one's actions is to assume a frightful burden," the warrior ant observed. "It is to accept responsibility for one's own fate. . . ."

Zorak nodded somberly. "That is true, Xikchaka, my friend. It is far easier to shrug off personal responsibility by saying you but followed the commands of your superior. But he may be your superior in rank, while remaining your inferior in intellect. It is in the nature of intelligent beings to desire to be the masters of their own fate. Any other condition, such as the servitude in which both Xikchaka and Zorak now toil, is slavery. And slavery is death to the will, to the mind, and to the spirit."

The insect warrior said slowly, "Is it not more comfortable to be protected, and to belong to a vast common purpose? The thing which Zorak calls 'freedom' sounds dangerous and lonely."

"It is," Zorak admitted firmly. "But there is more to life than merely to be comfortable. A baby in its mother's arms is comfortable and protected—or a grub, in the nesting place of a female. But to be a man, or a mature *kraan*, is better: and to be a man, in the truest sense of the word, is to be free. Which includes the freedom to be in danger or in discomfort."

"Xikchaka will never understand the ways of men," said the insect with a very human shaking of its immense, gleaming head.

They parted, then, without further words, and each pursued his own route.

That evening the ant horde halted in its march, for now it was only a branch-length away from the fork of the neighboring arboreal monarch in which Phaolon was built.

A *kraan* scouting party was sent out under Xikchaka from the parent body to investigate a small, artificial structure which was suspected to be of human workmanship. After a time, a scout returned to requisition a human captive, in order that the man might be questioned on the nature and purpose of the structure, as to whether or not it was an outpost of Phaolon, something in the nature of a watchtower, and perhaps inhabited by a body of armed human warriors.

As luck would have it, the man chosen for this purpose was Zorak the Bowman.

Under close guard, he ventured down the night-black branch until he came within sight of the artifact. It was a tower, the color of opals, which glowed softly with a gentle, all-pervasive luminance whose many hues were constantly shifting and changing, one color melting into another, like a ray of light directed to pass through a revolving prism.

From a forward vantage point, the scout ants observed the strange building while themselves remaining hidden behind a screen of foliage. Zorak was led forward until he, too, could observe the building unseen.

He found it curious and puzzling. It was patently obvious to the brawny bowman that the spire was not the work of human hands, or at least not the work of any civilization remotely akin to his own, for the design and fabrication of the tower, and the material from which it had been erected, was a complete mystery to him. Moreover, the building looked somehow deserted, although had you asked Zorak why he felt so, he could not have given you a reason.

"Is this a watchtower, guarding the approaches to Phaolon?" Xikchaka inquired in a rasping simulacrum of human speech.

Zorak was on the horns of a dilemma. In fact, he knew, or very strongly believed, that the Opal Tower was an artifact of one of the prehuman races which had formerly been the inhabitants of this planet. Since these races were known to be long extinct, he did not question that the tower was empty. However, he spoke up in equivocal terms, urging that the war party explore the structure, and did not give voice to his opinion as to its origin and history. From Zorak's point of view, every conceivable excuse to delay the advance of the horde in its march against Phaolon was legitimate and most desirable. Every hour that the horde remained stationary gave the folk of Niamh's city an extra margin of safety, and the opportunity to discover the *kraan* army before it attacked the outskirts of the city.

The ant warriors approached the base of the building with circumspection. The portal yawned widely open and unguarded.

They went in.

22.

Under the Knife

Within the Opal Tower the days passed slowly, and time seemed nonexistent. Niamh went about her waking hours in a manner which can only be described as somnambulistic. Her first fears that the dwarfed madman had preserved her for one of his horrible experiments seemed demonstrably false. She guessed that he reserved her for another purpose, one as yet unknowable.

Nightly he conversed with her through the concealed opening in her room, while Number Nine served her dinner on low tables inlaid with precious stones. Each of these nocturnal monologues was like a long, rambling dissertation by a brilliant but warped intelligence. Quoron described with feverish excitement the progress of his experiments, and announced that he was very close to achieving his ultimate goal, which was the severance of a human head in conjunction with the perfect preservation of all of its cognitive faculties.

On more than one of these occasions, Niamh thought that she glimpsed the flicker of awareness in the dull, glazed eyes of the many-limbed automaton. It was almost as if the double-headed monstrosity was capable of understanding the import of Quoron's conversation, and somehow remembered the operations which had served to render it the monstrosity it had become under his cunning knife.

For some reason which she could not explain, even to herself, that wan and feeble glimmer of understanding—almost of resentment—in the eyes of the monster gave her cause to hope. But to hope for what? She did not know.

Quoron appeared in her suite one evening, his hunched, diminutive form quivering with tension, his noble brow glistening with the perspiration of pure excitement.

"Tonight, young woman, you shall witness an event of unparalleled magnitude in the annals of scientific achievement!" the dwarf announced, his voice croaking and harsh with repressed eagerness.

"And what is that?" she inquired faintly. He lurched forward on bowed legs, thin lips fixed in a cold smile of triumph.

"My experiments have proved successful!" exulted the science wizard. "At last I have conquered the final obstacle in my path!"

"Do you mean you have discovered how to remove a human head without killing the brain?" asked Niamh, filled with apprehension. The dwarf leered with gloating in his eyes.

"No less than that," he crowed triumphantly. "It is now fully within my power to sever the braincase from the trunk while the brain retains its cognitive faculties unimpaired. An ingenious contrivance of my own design continues to supply oxygen to the brain-cells even after the major arteries have been disconnected. And in this historic experiment, you—*you!*—shall play a vital role. Your name shall not go unforgotten in the annals of our age, for you, my dear, shall witness the operation and shall bear your testimony to my achievement of the miracle to the civilizations of this planet!"

"But—who is to be the subject of the operation?" the girl faltered, faint with relief that this grim honor was not to fall to her.

"I, myself," exclaimed the cripple. "No longer shall I suffer the ignominy of possessing a brilliant intellect which is forced to go forever chained to this misshapen and revolting carcass! My head shall live on in solitary speculation, serenely aloof to the body, immortal—undying—godlike!"

"But who, then, will perform the operation?" the girl asked wonderingly. "Surely, it is not still your intention to permit this pitiful monstrosity to—to—?"

He chuckled. "Aye, but it is! Number Nine has been carefully trained and coached repeatedly in all steps of the process. With three hands at Nine's disposal, my faithful monster will be able to perform the most delicate of all surgical operations in a mere fraction of the time possible to an ordinary human."

With these words, the dwarf reached up, patting and stroking the motionless limbs of the immense creature which towered blank-eyed above him.

Niamh shuddered, but said nothing. A nameless foreboding filled her with apprehension. . . .

The operating theater was in readiness, and without further ado the fiendish experiment commenced. Quoron commanded his giant servant to chain the princess to the wall so that the girl could not possibly interfere during the procedures. Then he assumed his position on the white metal table under the glare of sterile lamps.

The ghoulish operation began.

First, the injection of a local anesthetic rendered Quoron totally insensible to pain. The dwarfed madman would remain fully conscious during every step of the process of decapitation.

Then, one by one, the hideous colossus severed the veins and arteries of the neck, attaching these to throbbing pumps by means of transparent tubes. Quoron explained that the device he called his "artificial heart" would monitor the circulation and purification of blood during the actual operation. Not for a single moment would his brain be deprived of its vital supply of freshly oxygenated blood.

Then Number Nine began severing the head of Quoron from his deformed body.

Several times during the process, Niamh averted her eyes in disgust and revulsion. But a sick fascination, for the most part, kept her attention to the incredible surgical feat.

For all its ghastly appearance and apparent idiocy, the four-armed monster had been meticulously trained. It was amazing to watch those uncouth limbs, performing miracles with the razor-thin scalpels, never faltering, never betraying their innate clumsiness for an instant.

Throughout the operation, the head of Quoron remained awake, following every step of the procedure with glittering eyes, although unable to speak or to comment until such time as the head was completely severed and its vocal organs were attached to the artificial breathing device which would make it possible for the decapitated head to make audible sounds again.

The final step—that of cutting through the spinal column—was performed with a small power saw. When the column was completely severed, the head was now independent of the body.

The last attachments were made. Number Nine stepped back as if to observe its grisly handiwork.

The head of Quoron hung in midair, supported by the various tubes and pipes which connected it to the life-support system. It smiled triumphantly at Niamh, thin, colorless lips drawing back from dry teeth in a rictus devoid of mirth. All that remained now was for Number Nine to attach the end of the air-hose to the stump of the neck, and the severed head could speak.

Number Nine returned the small saw to the tray of surgical implements, and reached for the organic jelly with which it would fasten the breathing apparatus to the head. But as it did so, its glazed eye was caught and held by a small and seemingly inoffensive piece of apparatus on the metal table.

This was a small tube of flame, resembling a Bunsen burner, in whose blaze the instruments had been sterilized.

Something flickered within the opaque eyes of the two-headed monster. Was it a wisp of memory—the residue of pain—recollection of that moment when its master, for an idle whim, had commanded it to hold its fingers in the flame of the candle in order to demonstrate to Niamh its complete helplessness to oppose the will of Quoron?

Perhaps. . . .

The lumbering giant stared at the naked flame and something like a whimper escaped from its lax, loosely open lips. An expression moved over the masculine head which was repeated, a few instants later, by the feminine head.

An expression of fear was followed by another expression, which was unreadable to Niamh.

In a moment, however, the twin brows were distorted in a double scowl, and the expression became discernible.

It was anger.

Quoron's eyes had followed this, and now they glittered with feverish impatience and with the first, faint stirrings of apprehension. Time and again the lips of the bodiless head opened as if to frame words, but no sound could escape from that twitching mouth, as yet unconnected to the air supply. The tongue came out and moistened dry lips, and again the mouth strove to frame a vocal command. But no words came from the helpless head.

While Niamh watched with shuddering revulsion, the monster bent over the equipment table, and carefully selected a long, thin-bladed knife.

Then it slowly approached the dangling head, the hilt of the knife clenched in its huge upper right hand.

While the eyes of Quoron widened in a fixed and ghastly stare of unbelieving, uncomprehending horror, the giant reached forward with the knife. Its four eyes glared down at the helpless head of its master. The expression in those eyes astonished the princess, for the eyes of Number Nine now mirrored neither hatred nor anger nor even rage.

Their gaze was the cold, thoughtful, level, measuring look that appears in the eyes of a judge as he calmly ponders the fate of a despicable criminal.

Then the hand which held the knife lifted, drew back, and plunged the blade to its hilt into Quoron's brain.

23.

Unexpected Meetings

The decision which Varda reached was the only one possible to one of her temperament. Madly infatuated with me, she could not endure the idea of slaying me herself; but neither could she permit me to escape without her. So she set me free.

Donning my garments and resuming my weapons, which she had kept stored in her cabin, I was soon ready to depart. Indeed every moment counted, for even now the vindictive Iona must be halfway back to Varda's cabin, at the head of the troop of girls.

Together, Varda and I propped open the rear window—the same one through which Iona had spied upon us only minutes earlier. I lifted the slender girl over the sill and vaulted through the opening as soon as she was clear of it. Hand in hand we crept through the gloom of darkness, seeking the place where the wild girls had tethered my sky-sled to the farther side of the branch.

I could not see my hand in front of my face, so deep and thick was the unbroken blackness of the night. But Varda knew every step of the way, and guided us with swift, unerring skill to the spot.

Examining the vehicle, I was relieved to learn that the teen-aged savages had merely emptied the sled of its stores, but had not tampered with either the controls or the engines. I lifted Varda aboard and showed her how to

strap herself into one of the long shallow troughlike depressions scooped out in the shape of a human body.
Then, assuming the pilot's position, I energized the vehicle, and drew in the anchor-line that held us fastened to
the twig. By the time Iona had burst triumphantly into
Varda's cabin, to find the surprise of her life, we had
glided away from the limb and soon became lost in the
dense gloom.

It is dangerous to fly by night through the world-forest,
because of the dangers of collision with a branch or bole,
and the ever-present hazards of becoming enmeshed in
one of the monster spider webs spun between the giant
trees by the immense albino spiders the Laonese call
the *xoph*. So we flew only as far as the adjoining branch
before tethering our craft in a safe place.

Or, at least, in a place we assumed to be safe.

With dawn we had a surprise of our own, however; and
it was every bit as much of a shock as the jolt our inexplicable absence probably gave to Iona.

When the *kraan* scouting party burst into the gleaming
white room under the blaze of the sterile lamps, they beheld an unfathomable tableau.

Suspended amid a maze of pipes and flexible tubing,
the lifeless head of a noble-looking man hung with a
scalpel thrust directly between its eyes.

Shackled to the farther wall, a slim, exquisite young
woman stared at them with eyes wide and frightened in
the tense white oval of her face.

From a distant chamber came the sound of shattering
glass and the crash of overturned tables. A moment later
there appeared in the doorway a towering colossus with
four arms, three legs, and two heads, brandishing a length
of metallic tubing.

It was Number Nine.

After wreaking a dire but deserved vengeance upon its
mad creator, the shambling horror had run amok. First it

had gone on a rampage through the outer laboratory, smashing the vessels which held in a ghastly semblance of vitality the several organs removed from human bodies, which Quoron had striven to imbue with life.

Then it entered the white chamber and put the idiot head of Wa-Wa out of its misery.

Now it burst into the operation theater and charged the ant scouts, waving its improvised metal club. The berserk giant went crashing through the great warrior ants, hurling them aside, shattering their carapaces of horny chitin with terrific blows, swinging its metal club with irresistible force.

The *kraan,* their antennae jerking in agitation, withdrew from the chamber, forcing Zorak to accompany them. Crowded together in the narrow corridor, the ant warriors could not easily bring into play their mighty pincers or the fierce claws with which their multiple-jointed limbs were armed. One by one they died under the blows of the mad giant's club, but not before their sharp, toothed mandibles had wrought savage wounds in the torso and arms of the colossus, which soon streamed blood from a dozen injuries.

Clustering at the base of the tower, Xikchaka dispatched two ant warriors and Zorak the Bowman to rejoin the main body of the horde and report their discovery.

They had not got far from the site of the Opal Tower, however, before a new marvel burst upon them in the form of a tall, gaunt, naked manlike figure with leathery golden hide and immense batwings.

It was Zarqa the Kalood!

One of the ant warriors thrust the long spear it held at the weird figure as it hovered on flapping, ungainly wings two yards above the branch's surface. The Winged Man reached out with long arms and snatched the weapon from the grip of the *kraan* who was jabbing it in his direction.

Then, with miraculous precision, Zarqa flung the heavy spear directly at the great red ant, transfixing its body. So powerful was the impetus of his spear-cast that the spear not only penetrated the *kraan* chitinous armor, but pierced its body, pinning it to the branch to which it clung with many feet.

Simultaneously, Zorak, instantly recognizing the gaunt Kalood as a friend, turned on the second ant scout, jerked his tether from its claws, and sprang upon its back. While sharp horny mandibles chomped and scraped against his burly forearm, the stalwart bowman thrust one arm between the jaws of the huge insect, seized its hooked snout in the other hand, and with one surge of massive thews, broke its neck.

Twitching spasmodically, the scarlet monster collapsed, and Zorak sprang free. Snatching away his choke collar, the brawny bowman drew his first deep breath as a free man in many days.

The Kalood came down to a fluttering landing on the branch and in a moment they clasped hands in heartfelt greeting.

I had not expected to find you, bowman, said the Winged Man in his solemn telepathic mode of speech, which was like a small quiet voice speaking amid your own thoughts.

"But I am very glad you did!" Zorak said feelingly, grinning. "Two against one are very unequal odds, especially when the two are great killer *kraan*."

I was searching by mental means for my lost companions, continued Zarqa, *and it seemed to me that I detected the radiations of the mind of Princess Niamh, which were emanating from a tower of my race very near to where we are standing. Flying toward the spire I observed you being led along the branch by these two insect creatures, and could not afford to let pass the opportunity of rescuing you, as well.*

"For which I confess myself extremely grateful." Zorak

smiled. "And you are indeed correct: the princess is bound to an upper chamber within the tower, which lies a ways farther up the branch from here. My *kraan* captors and I were just returning to the main body of the ant-army to summon reinforcements to surround the tower, which is held by a murdering monster with an unusual assortment of arms, legs, and heads."

Then it is imperative that we repair to the tower at once, in order to rescue the princess from the clutches of the ogre you describe, commented Zarqa.

Zorak heartily agreed. Taking up the weapons with which the two ants had been armed, he and the Winged Man headed at once for the tower of Quoron.

But they were too late. . . .

After the berserk giant had driven the giant ants from the laboratory, leaving her alone and still helplessly manacled to the wall, Niamh sagged wearily in her chains, pondering the peculiar reverses of fortune. Had it not been Zorak the Bowman she had, however briefly, glimpsed at the rear of the ant party when they had entered the chamber? She could have sworn it was indeed the gallant Tharkoonian archer who had so recklessly sprung to her assistance many days ago in Komar, when the sky craft drifted free of the palace roof.

Relieved as she was to discover that the stalwart bowman had somehow survived his fall from the branch, after their battle with the dragonlike *ythid,* the spirits of the princess wilted within her as he was snatched from her sight again by the monster insects, who seemed to be his masters.

Now she was alone in the Opal Tower with a raving maniac!

It was a situation so dire and perilous as to dishearten even the most sanguine of heroines. But there was more to come, as Niamh soon discovered.

For she was not alone. . . .

Appearing as suddenly as an apparition, the huge form

of a mighty insect filled the doorway to the operating theater.

The red ant stood observing her from its featureless casque of a head with multicellular eyes like enormous, many-faceted black crystals. No human emotion was readable in the cold glitter of those uncanny eyes.

Beneath its head, a low-slung jaw moved slightly. Saw-toothed mandibles rasped against each other in a slow, rubbing motion which sent a thrill of fearful anticipation through the girl's slight frame.

Many-jointed feet moved spiderwise. Claws clicking against the white tiles of the floor, the gigantic killer ant moved slowly into the room.

The glare of sterilizing lamps gleamed on the oily red chitin armor that entirely covered its swelling thorax.

While Niamh watched, eyes fixed in fascination upon the silent monster, it approached the wall to which she was chained, moving gradually. The stealthy, almost furtive, way in which it advanced upon her reminded the helpless girl of the manner in which a cunning tree-dragon stealthily creeps upon its unsuspecting prey.

Across the upper breast of the monster *kraan* inexplicable signs or markings were painted. Several of its minor limbs grasped edged metal weapons. From these two facts, and the orderly manner in which the party of ants had withdrawn from the room before the charging colossus, the girl deduced that the giant insect was of coldly unhuman intelligence.

But having never seen a specimen of the *kraan* so closely before, she had no way of guessing its mood or its purpose.

She watched with eyes wide in hypnotic fascination as the enormous insect came within a few feet of where she was bound.

Then it reached with clawed limbs for her, and she screamed.

24.

The Kiss

The great ant reached for her and Niamh screamed and shrank against the wall. Grasping her binding chains in its claws, the *kraan* thrust its head forward and crunched the links of the chain between its horny mandibular jaws.

After several tries, the *kraan* succeeded in biting through the chain.

And Niamh was free. . . .

She stared with unbelieving eyes at the giant insect as it assisted her in stripping away the last vestiges of her bondage. Then, rasping and clicking its mandibles together in a weird and, at first, unintelligible imitation of human speech, the warrior ant addressed the girl it had set free.

"Once a male member of your species assisted Xikchaka to freedom from bondage," the insect-creature said. "Later, we assisted each other in the wilderness; but Xikchaka's human companion was captured by the warriors and scouts of Xikchaka's own kind. In memory of the kindness which a member of your species once performed for this unworthy and ungrateful *kraan*, Xikchaka has served you as the human, Zorak, served Xikchaka."

"Thank you for your kindness," whispered Niamh faintly. The insect-creature regarded her with solemn, emotionless gaze. Then it slowly shook its huge helmlike head from side to side in a negative gesture obviously copied from humans.

"It is not 'kindness,' " said the great ant. "The *kraan* do not understand such human emotions as the one called 'kindness.' No; it is simply logical for Xikchaka to do this. A returned favor balances the score. Perhaps, at some period in the unguessable future, Xikchaka will be in a difficult or a dangerous position, and you will be able to lend him aid. Go, now, to that freedom which it seems you humans prize so highly. The night is dark. Xikchaka's fellow *kraan* will not be able to observe you pass, for he has commanded them to withdraw from the vicinity of the tower into a place of concealment. As for the deformed human giant, it has been slain. Go, then. But if ever in your wanderings you encounter a male of your species, one Zorak by name, say to him that perhaps he has been instrumental in teaching one *kraan,* at least, the meaning of 'friendship.' "

Niamh went, and speedily, fleeing from the tower and down the branch in the darkness to the place where she had left the sky-ship of Ralidux.

Thus it ocurred that when Zarqa the Kalood and Zorak the Bowman came to the Opal Tower they found it untenanted by anyone save the dead.

Among them, the body of Niamh of Phaolon, happily, was not to be found. Neither were the remainder of the scouting party, or Xikchaka. Thus it was that the two had no notion of what had become of the princess nor of where she had fled.

Do not worry, friend Zorak, the Winged Man reassured his comrade. *She cannot have gone far on foot, and by mind-search I shall soon locate her.*

"That is all very well, since you have wings, but I must go on foot," remarked the bowman. "We must part here, I am afraid. If you manage to find the princess, tell her that the ant horde is under the insidious influence of Delgan, the former Warlord of the Blue Barbarians, and that it is poised to march against Niamh's own city of Phaolon, which cannot lie more than a tree or two away from this branch. Alert the warriors of Phaolon, I beg you!"

We shall carry the warning to them together, you and I, advised Zarqa with a slight smile. *For, having once located you, it is not my intention to permit us to become separated again. My wings are as strong as they are swift, and I can easily bear your weight for a time.*

So saying, the tall Kalood bent and picked up the bowman. Spreading his batlike wings, Zarqa sprang lightly into the air to resume his mental quest.

Niamh found to her delighted surprise that the vessel remained exactly at the place where she had left it, and had seemingly not been tampered with during her absence. Entering the cabin of the craft the girl examined the controls, anxious to be gone before other members of the ant horde might come upon her and make her their captive.

Tugging at the levers and thrusting the control studs at random, the girl struggled to find the secret of driving the aerial vehicle which earlier had eluded her. After some experimentation, she at last discovered the correct combination of actions by which she was able to energize the sky craft, and she sent it gliding into the air.

The darkness of night was still upon the world, but Niamh knew there were only a few hours until dawn. Reaching the tree nearest to the one in which she had been held captive in the Opal Tower by Quoron, she tethered the vehicle to a twig and composed herself for a brief period of slumber until dawn should drive away the dark and make further flight possible.

She could not have guessed the astounding sight her eyes would behold with the break of day.

Varda and I had taken refuge from the night in the branches of a giant tree. Here we decided to spend the remainder of the night, to fly on with morning.

We were in no danger from pursuit by the angry and vengeful girls of Varda's band. The Amazon girls had neither *zaiph* nor *dhua* and thus could not follow us between the trees.* This fact notwithstanding, I was in considerable danger from Varda, for the impetuous and amorous teen-ager insisted on snuggling up next to me while we slept the remainder of the night away.

More than once I half awoke from a doze to find her warm arms entwined about my neck. I would, on these occasions, disengage myself as gently as was possible without disturbing her. And once I woke to find her head buried in my shoulder. The warm fragrance of her breath caressed my nostrils.

I felt distinctly uncomfortable, and heartily wished for dawn.

When the first beams of the Green Star began to lighten the nocturnal gloom, we roused ourselves from our rest and prepared to resume our aerial journey. But Varda was in an obstinate mood. She pouted and glowered and refused to permit me to take off from the bough until I granted her one request.

I did not require the humid gleam in her eyes to tell me the nature of that request.

I tried to be firm.

"Listen to me, girl," I said in a low voice. "I have already told you that I cannot love you, for my heart is foresworn and I am vowed to another. The most we can ever be is good friends. Varda, do not make our hazardous journey even more uncomfortable by insisting

* The *zaiph* are gigantic dragonflies, tamed for the purpose of riding by the Laonese; *dhua* are immense gauzy-winged moths, used by the humans of this planet to draw their aerial chariots.
—*Editor.*

upon that which can never be! Try to understand that I love another girl, and must ever be true to her."

"But—!"

"You are no longer the master of the situation, nor am I any longer your slave, and thus obedient to your every whim," I reminded her. "The situation is now more or less reversed: I am the master of this vessel, and you must do as I say."

"Very well, Karn," she said meekly. Then: "Oh, Karn ..."

I sighed vexedly.

"What is it?"

"I will annoy you no further," she said in a small voice. "I ask only one favor of you . . . small recompense, indeed, for my having freed you and assisted you to escape. One thing only do I beg of you."

"Very well; what is it?"

"A kiss," she whispered. "Only one kiss . . . a little one, at that. To remember you by. . . ."

I should not, of course, have given in to her wheedling, but I did. After all, she had set me loose, and fled with me, giving up everything she had possessed, her friends, her position as chieftainess, all for me. I sighed and yielded to her coaxing.

"Very well, then, but only one. Come here."

She came joyously into my arms and her slim, vibrant body nestled within the circle of my embrace. She tilted her head to meet my lips, and her mouth was warm and tender and sweet, I kissed her quite thoroughly.

Then she broke off the kiss, stiffening in my arms with a sharp little cry.

I glanced around behind me—

Niamh woke from her slumbers as the first beams of dawn touched her lids. For a moment she did not recognize her surroundings and gazed about her, wonderingly. Then, remembering the grisly succession of recent events, she shuddered, yawned, stretched, and got to her feet.

The faint murmur of voices came to her and she froze. The voices—there were two of them—were pitched too low for her to make out the words.

Peering about, she found that she had moored the aerial craft near the terminus of one mighty bough, where the branch divided into numerous twigs from which sprang gigantic golden leaves. These leaves effectively screened from her view whatever lay on the other side.

Anxious to discover the identity of the other persons who shared this part of the branch with her, she parted the leaves and peered through at a curious scene.

Tethered to one twig floated a strangely shaped metal craft.

Standing close together on the deck of this weightless vehicle were the half-naked figures of a young boy about her own age, with shoulder-length hair the color of raw gold. His broad and suntanned back was turned to her and Niamh could not see his features.

He was holding in his arms a slim young girl perhaps a few years younger than himself. As Niamh watched, the two embraced and kissed tenderly.

Suddenly, the girl cried out and pulled away, staring at Niamh's face through the leaves. The boy turned around and looked to see what had frightened her.

I stared at Niamh incredulously, my face crimsoning. The features of my long-lost, beloved princess whitened slowly, as the color drained from them. Her eyes were wide, and filled with shock, with hurt, and with disbelief.

Then they filled with tears. With a cold expression of disdain, Niamh looked me up and down, and turned away.

25.

The Ending of It

With dawn the sentinels perched high aloft in the tallest towers of Phaolon discovered the advance of the crawling horde of scarlet *kraan*. In their countless thousands the giant warrior ants approached the edges of the Jewel City, brandishing their glittering weapons.

Although taken completely by surprise, the Phaolonese were swift to arm themselves for the conflict. Silver-throated trumpets rang from the tower-tops, and the warriors of the city donned their lacquered mail, took up their slim lances, and belted their swords to their sides. Then, clambering into the saddles of their great war-*zaiphs*, they soared in steeply ascending spirals, and darted down upon the vangard of the *kraan* horde.

Their metal sparkling in the glowing shafts of emerald radiance that streamed between the mighty boles of the world-forest, pennons of brilliant hues fluttering from the tips of their spears, mounted on immense insects with stiff wings like sheeted opals, the chevaliers of Phaolon resembled so many elfin knights flashing through the air on winged steeds to do battle with some goblin army which had crept upon them in the night, invading Fairyland.

The Phaolonese warriors had the advantage of being able to strike from aloft, while the crawling ants were earthbound. But, although the shining lances and keen-edged swords of the cavaliers cut a terrible swath through the outer fringes of the advancing horde, the *kraan* were as numberless as the leaves of the trees. For every warrior ant which fell before the flying knights, there were a dozen ready to take its place.

Several disadvantages fought against the side of the folk of Phaolon, and the worst of them all was that the Jewel City had no walls to protect it from an invasion. This was only natural and understandable, since the humans who dwelt in the world-forest used aerial steeds, and no city can wall itself against an attack from the air. Now this factor weighed heavily against Niamh's people, for soon the first squadrons of the ant horde were among the houses built upon the outskirts of the city, and were crawling down the narrow streets, slaughtering everyone they encountered. The flying warriors could not defend the streets of Phaolon from above with any facility, due to the breadth of the *zaiphs'* wings.

In the center of the horde stood Delgan, a smile of aloof amusement on his thin lips, as he watched the invasion. All of this he had carefully foreseen, and thus far it was going according to his plans. Beside him crouched the gigantic figure of the ant monarch, Rkhith, his immense and many-legged form glittering with bejeweled trappings.

The battle progressed. Despite everything the aerial knights of Phaolon could do to prevent them, the forefront of the insect invasion poured into the streets of the city.

Before long it would be all over, Delgan knew. And he smiled at the thought.

Then something happened which Delgan had not foreseen. Down through the morning sky hurtled a gleaming metallic craft bearing a boy and a girl. The girl Delgan did not know, but the boy he knew all too well, and he ground his teeth together in rage at his untimely appearance.

It was Karn, with Varda beside him, on the sky-sled.

"Delgan and the *kraan* horde."

The ant warriors recoiled at the sudden appearance of this strange flying vehicle, and while they hesitated in their advance, a second sky craft materialized above the crowded streets of Phaolon. This one was piloted by a young woman who was also known to Delgan—Niamh the Fair!

The two aerial vessels skimmed low over the streets, and the ant horde cringed beneath the shadows of their keels, and became disorganized and jammed together so that they could hardly move, as the *kraan* behind pressed forward into the ranks of those in the forefront of the assault.

While this momentary congestion lasted, while the advancing warrior ants hesitated to eye these flying vehicles with trepidation and alarm, the archers of Phaolon seized the moment to pour their feathered shafts into the packed mass of ants. The barbed hail swept through the horde and took a ghastly toll of the attackers, for so tightly were the *kraan* jammed together that virtually every shaft loosed from the bows of Phaolon transfixed the head or thorax of an ant warrior.

As soon as the attackers managed to overcome their momentary hesitation, and began to disentangle themselves and to press forward again, yet a third flying enemy appeared in the air above the beleaguered city. This one was the most peculiar of them all—a batwinged, naked, golden man with a burly warrior in his arms. It was none other than Zarqa the Kalood, with Zorak of Tharkoon.

The Tharkoonian had recovered his bow and quiver of arrows from the Opal Tower, for Quoron had stored the weapon away when he had relieved Niamh of it in her dungeon cell while she slept. And the mighty bow soon wreaked a fearful toll of *kraan*. Flying above the host of swarming scarlet insects, Zarqa and Zorak fought as a team, the telepathic Kalood discerning the officers of the horde by mental means, and calling Zorak's attention to these. The bowman then slew them one by one, while

Zarqa flew high above, well out of reach of the weapons of the *kraan*.

The social system under which the insect-creatures toiled exposed its most crippling flaw then.

True, Zorak had guessed the identity of that innate weakness in the *kraan* civilization early on, but now it became obvious to all.

With their superiors and commanders slain by Zorak's bow, the ant warriors milled about, dazed and bewildered, unable to adjust to a change in the situation of the moment, and unwilling to act on their own initiative.

Without their officers to tell them what to do, the warrior ants were confused and helpless.

Sensing this, both Karn and Niamh landed their flying vehicles atop the tall buildings and took aboard as many of the Phaolonese archers as their craft could carry.

Then they flew out over the thronged streets again, firing a deadly storm of arrows down into the staggering, entangled, befuddled *kraan*.

Taking heart, the armored chivalry of Phaolon, the princess and warriors and nobles, the yeomen and the guardsmen, too, charged down the streets of the city to hew a crimson path deep into the heart of the ant invasion.

Simultaneously under attack from above and from their fore, the warrior *kraan* could think of nothing else but to turn back, and regroup, and await new orders. But the ant warriors in the rear continued to crawl forward in obedience to the last orders they had been given. In no time they were hopelessly jammed together, as the front ranks tried to retreat. Soon, they were so closely packed together, that they could not move in either direction.

The archers in the sky-sled and the other craft, and Zorak's mighty bow, and the flying cavalry of Phaolon, swept them with a barbed storm of death, again and again.

They died in their hundreds, and in their thousands.

And even Xikchaka saw the evidence of Zorak's arguments, and knew the human had spoken the truth.

Sensing the inevitability of defeat, Rkhith wheeled about and commanded his retinue of advisers and senior officers and his personal guards to retreat. Delgan, however, refused. The blue-skinned man was in a frenzy, his lean, aristocratic features distorted in a feral snarl, his skin glistening with cold perspiration, the glint of maniacal fury in his eyes. In one hand he brandished the *zoukar,* the death-flash, which he had stolen from the boy Karn long ago, and to which he had clung all this while.

"Do not flee," he panted. "All is not lost. Listen to me, you crawling fool! With this I can bring down the aerial warriors, and the day is yet ours—"

But Rkhith was beyond the reach of argument or reason. The giant *kraan* had never before known the acrid taste of fear, but he knew it now, and he did not care for the taste of it. Cold logical thinking had deserted him, and the most primal of the emotions now reigned in its stead. The insect monster, in his frenzied haste to be gone from this scene of incredible carnage, did not recognize the wily human who had insidiously worked his way into Rkhith's inner councils. He knew only that a despised human blocked his path.

The many-jointed limbs of Rkhith were armed with terrible claws and pincers. These reached out and seized upon the wild-eyed man. Cruelly sinking their saw-teeth into his flesh, they lifted his writhing, kicking form high into the air, and cast him to one side. Then Rkhith crawled hastily farther down the vast bough, at whose base the sparkling spires and domes of Phaolon were built, and fled.

But not very far.

Streaming with gore from his many wounds, Delgan levered himself up into a sitting position from where he had been flung, and with shaking hands aimed the *zoukar* after the fleeing form of his one-time master.

The bolt of lightning struck Rkhith from behind, with a sizzling flash of electric fire that momentarily lighted the air to intolerable brilliance.

A wriggling mass of seething flames, the king-ant died. Crisped and blackened, his corpse rolled down the steep side of the branch and feel to the unknown floor of the forest far below.

Sagging back, Delgan uttered one wry, croaking laugh. Then blood gushed from between his grinning jaws and his eyes went dead and empty, and he sprawled lifeless, the *zoukar* still clutched tight in his hand.

They had to pry his fingers apart to recover the death-flash, when they found the body. . . .

In this manner the invasion of Phaolon was ended.

And so—almost—is my tale.

The Aftermath

And so it was that, in the moment of its greatest peril, Niamh and Zarqa and Zorak and Varda and I appeared, to turn the tide of the battle.

With the scarlet horde decimated, its broken remnants fleeing in disorganized retreat, we landed our aerial vessels upon the steps of the palace to receive the hysterical plaudits of the victorious throng.

Men and women wept openly at the sight of their beloved princess, lost to them so very long, and now miraculously returned in the very hour of their supreme need.

The lords and courtiers of the palace pressed around Niamh, tears of joy coursing down their cheeks, to wrap her slim form in sumptuous robes of crimson, and to set upon her small proud head the glittering coronet of royalty. Many among them I recognized, having known them during my previous incarnation as Chong the Mighty. Among these was the old sage and philosopher of the court, Khin-nom, wah had taught me the language of the Laonese.

But, of course, they did not know me. It is beyond the ability of men to recognize a spirit clothed in a new body.

After greeting her courtiers and accepting their homage, Niamh turned to thank us for our aid. She stood on tiptoes to place a chaste kiss on the gaunt, leathery cheek of the solemn-eyed Kalood, and for one moment I thought I glimpsed a very human emotion in the eyes of the Winged Man.

Zorak knelt and kissed her hand, and she raised the stalwart bowman to his feet and proclaimed him a knight-baronet of Phaolon. She even spoke briefly with Varda, and the girl was shy and blushing at suddenly being surrounded with such magnificence. But she whispered a terse message in the ears of my beloved, who as yet had not given me so much as a single glance. How I regretted having yielded so foolishly to Varda's plea! Then Niamh and Varda parted, having exchanged a brief conversation. Niamh seemed flushed and starry-eyed, and Varda gave me a look that was demure, yet conspiratorial.

What was the headstrong, impetuous, infatuated girl up to now? Hadn't she done enough to destroy my hopes for happiness?

Niamh came over to where I stood, and took me by the hand, rather surprisingly, and led me before the assembled throng.

"Greet the young hero who is to become your prince—and my husband," she said.

There was a moment of silence. The Phaolonese seemed shocked, but not one of them was as surprised as I was. Then they burst into cheers, and Niamh looked at me, with a tender and tremulous smile.

"Varda has told me the true story of the intimate scene I witnessed this morning," said my beloved in a small voice. "I should never have doubted for one moment your love for she whom you once knew as 'Shann of Kamadhong.' Can you find it in your heart to forgive me, Karn?"

For answer I swept her into my arms and there, before the vast assemblage, I kissed her most thoroughly indeed.

Thus was my world won back for me, now and forever mine.

There was one question left unanswered, and it was wise old Khin-nom who put it into words for the rest of us.

"I still do not understand why the center of the *kraan* horde broke and crumbled so swiftly into a milling and disorganized throng," he murmured, "when the aerial attack was inflicting heavy losses only on the forefront of the attack."

Zorak smiled and supplied us with the answer.

"Xargo the smith and I arranged the diversion long before," admitted the bowman. "We had been laboring to complete weapons for the *kraan*; while so engaged, we also manufactured weapons with which to arm the human slaves held in bondage to the horde. When the attack was blunted by Phaolonese resistance, and by our triple assault from the air, Xargo seized the momentary distraction of the horde chiefs to launch the slave revolt we had planned." And, without further ado, he brought forward the burly and battered and blushing figure of the smith, Xargo, whom Niamh ennobled for his part in the great victory.

It must be related here that our flying troops followed the fleeing *kraan* and negotiated with their new leader, that same Xikchaka who had freed Niamh from her chains, the release of all human captives and a vow never again to attack the cities of men, in return for our permission to let the surviving *kraan* escape the tree. We could otherwise have continued to pursue and slay them until the entire horde was destroyed.

These assurances Xikchaka solemnly gave us, and in greeting his former comrade, Zorak, the warrior ant acknowledged that his criticisms of the weaknesses inherent in the rigidly authoritarian ant civilization had been demonstrably accurate.

"From now on, Zorak, know that under the chieftaincy of Xikchaka, individual initiative and freedom of choice will be encouraged. Never again will the horde of

Xikchaka take human slaves, nor attempt to attack a settlement of men. There is room enough, and more, on this world, for both human beings and the *kraan* to mutually coexist without conflict."

With those words they parted, and Xikchaka led his folk farther into the world-forest, having surrendered all captives.

Our victory left us with many things yet to accomplish. Niamh dispatched Zorak and Zarqa in the sky-ship, requesting them to return to the isle of Komar and assist Prince Janchan, Princess Arjala, and my old comrade-in-arms, Klygon the Assassin, to join us in Phaolon.

Then Niamh herself, accompanied by the maid Varda and Arjala, flew in the sky-ship to the camp of the girl savages. They managed to persuade the Amazon girls to accept Phaolon's offer of assistance; some of the girls wished to return to their former homes in the city of Barganath, to which they were flown on *zaiph*-back under the escort of a full company of the flying Phaolonese cavalry; others, however, decided to accept Niamh's gracious invitation to come back to Phaolon with her, and find new homes and new friends at court.

The wild girls are settling in nicely, and are beginning to lose their savage ways.

Varda has become one of my wife's ladies-in-waiting. Changeful and mercurial as ever, the impetuous girl has now conceived of a furious passion for Zorak, and the stalwart bowman is hard put to resist her enticements and blandishments. Since the women of the Laonese marry quite young, as in India, it is quite possible that the former Tharkoonian will not long persist in keeping the willful girl at arm's length, and Zorak and Varda may, before long, follow Niamh and I to the altar.

Yes, we are husband and wife at last, my beloved and I. We were wed in the great throneroom of Phaolon by the high-priest, Lord Eloigam, before a mighty throng which numbered in the thousands. All of my dear friends were there to witness our long-delayed nuptials, those who had fought at my side during innumerable adventures—Zarqa the Kalood and Klygon the Assassin, Prince Janchan and his mate, the Goddess Arjala, Zorak the Bowman and the maiden, Varda. As well, Prince Andar the Komarian attended the festivities, with a retinue of his nobles, those who had toiled with us at the oars of the slaveship *Xothun*.

The ceremonies ended; I gathered my dear one into my arms, and sealed our nuptials with a kiss. Then swords flashed from a thousand scabbards, and all that mighty throng knelt in one flourish, saluting me as their Prince and ruler . . . and I discovered that the Laonese have no concept such as that of prince-consort: to wed the regnant Princess of Phaolon is to become a king!

Soon we departed on our honeymoon to a small villa built high in the branches of the great tree which houses our kingdom. Of our first days—and nights—of life together as man and wife, I will say nothing. Some memories are too precious to be put into words. My reader, if ever he has loved and wed, will understand my reticence.

There but remained one final task which I felt I must perform. And now it, too, is concluded.

I have placed the body of Prince Karn in a trance of suspended animation, by the employment of those arts of self-hypnotism I mastered long ago. Then, detaching my spirit from its clay, I returned across the vast reaches of the Universe to the planet of my birth, and resumed the body in which I had been born a hopeless cripple.

In the days and weeks since I recovered consciousness in my ancestral home in Connecticut, I have compiled this record of my adventures on the World of the Green Star. And now, at last, my history is finished. Surely, it must stand among the annals of adventure as one of the most astounding narratives of quest and peril and exploration ever lived.

Only a few minutes remain to me on this Earth.

Soon I shall quit forever the body in which my spirit was born. This record shall be sealed away in a bank vault until such time as the last spark of life has faded within my poor, weak, crippled body, and the executors of my estate determine (if indeed they ever do) that this narrative should be delivered into the hands of a publisher.

Soon—soon!—I shall wing my way across the starry space again, to the World of the Green Star.

Here on Earth I am a helpless cripple, unable to tend to my needs or take a single step unaided.

But there, on the World of the Green Star, I am a warrior and a hero, a husband, a lover, and a king. Never thereafter shall I wander the starry firmament again. For, on that weird and terrible and beautiful and wonder-filled planet of strange beasts and even stranger men, I found my heart's home.

I am caught in the Green Star's spell.

Nor do I wish ever to be freed from that sorcery.

Editor's Note

and
Appendix

Editor's Note

Mr. Donald A. Wollheim
DAW Books, Inc.
1301 Avenue of the Americas
New York, New York 10019

June 11, 1975

Dear Don:

Unless the post office has goofed again, you should find enclosed herewith a bundle of manuscript which I have entitled *In the Green Star's Spell*. I hope you find it as enthralling to read as I did. As was the case with the four volumes which preceded it, I have ever-so-slightly edited ————'s journals, dividing the narrative into chapters, giving them, and the book itself) a title, and making minor alterations in spelling, grammar, and punctuation.

I have also compiled a glossary of the characters in the five books, which I have tacked on as an appendix. By this time the saga—which is really one huge connected story—has run to considerably more than a quarter of a million words, and has become so complicated, with such an immense cast of characters, that I felt such a glossary was necessary for the readers' ease and convenience.

This is the last Green Star book, I'm afraid.

The trustees of ————'s estate informed me, when

they forwarded this part of the journals for me to edit, that this was the fifth and last notebook in the safe-deposit box. Further questioning elicited some information previously not disclosed to me in regard to the background of the narrative. About three years ago, after a previous but much briefer attack of similar nature, ——— fell into an extended coma lasting some weeks, during which he was kept alive only by intravenous feeding, all efforts to revive him having failed.

After weeks in this trancelike state, he "returned to himself," and began to write these journals. The first volume of the journals—*Under the Green Star*—he had written after coming out of the first trance. Finishing four new volumes of the narrative while recuperating in his ancestral home in rural Connecticut near the town of Harriton, he ordered that all five volumes be sealed in a bank vault, and again passed into the trancelike condition. Physicians say the state resembles catatonia; all life-functions continue to operate, but at minimal levels.

He remained in this comatose state for the better part of a year, and then died quietly in his sleep, despite all efforts by the Extensive Care Unit of Harriton Emergency Hospital doctors and staff to keep him alive. Upon his demise, lawyers from the firm of Brinton, Brinton, and Carruthers opened the box and discovered the journals, which were passed along to me through the advice of Tom Anderson. The rest of the story you know. . . .

So now we have reached the bottom of the cache of manuscripts, and there is nothing more to be added to the saga. It would seem that, after his marriage to Niamh the Fair, ——— returned to Earth briefly, for no other reason than to record an account of his adventures, before leaving his body again to return to the Green Star. This time for good.

Last weekend, after completing my work on the fifth book and handing it over to my typist, Scott and I drove up to Harriton and visited ————'s home. He is buried in the family plot, you know, there on the estate.

I stood for a few moments before his grave, and the thoughts which passed through my mind were concerned with the mystery of his secret. For only he knows whether the narratives were truth or fiction. If fiction, they are excellent enough; but if true, they comprise the most fantastic saga of adventure any human being has ever lived. And I—even I—do not know whether they are truth or fiction.

That secret he has carried with him to his grave.

Or . . . beyond! To a mist-veiled world of mighty trees that is bathed in the emerald radiance of the Green Star. . . .

Who knows? Certainly not I.

> Best wishes to Elsie and
> to Betsy,
>
> LIN

P.S. My friend Ken Franklin of the Hayden Planetarium tells me that no green star is known to exist in the entire universe.

Personally, I think he's full of hooey. What do *you* think?

Appendix:

The People of the Green Star World

> *Note:* By this fifth book in the Saga of the Green Star the story has become such a complex tapestry, comprised of so many interwoven strands of plot, peopled with so many characters, that I believe the following glossary will help explicate the relationships of the characters. In the interests of brevity, I have eliminated some minor figures of only peripheral consequence.
>
> —*L. C.*

AKHMIM OF ARDHA: Tyrant-Prince of Phaolon's neighboring city, who in the first two books poses the threat of invasion and war against Niamh's realm.

PRINCE ANDAR: Hereditary monarch of the island-city of Komar, whom Karn first meets in the fourth book, when they are fellow galley slaves aboard the *Xothun*.

ARJALA: The living Goddess of Ardha, whom Janchan wins for his mate.

ATHGAR: The forest savage who is Karn's father; a subchieftain of the Red Dragon nation.

BARYLLUS: High Priest of Karoga, the many-armed god of the Komarians.

CHONG THE MIGHTY: A legendary hero of ancient Phaolon, whose magically preserved body serves as the

186

first incarnation of the hero of the Saga of the Green Star. At the end of the first book of the saga, he is slain by Sligon the Betrayer.

CLYON: A superior savant of the Skymen of Calidar; one of the Pallicratian faction.

DELGAN OF THE ISLES: Warlord of the Blue Barbarians, whom Karn and Klygon befriend during their captivity in the cave-world. Together they gain freedom and reach the Komarian Sea, whereupon Delgan steals their craft and weapons, abandoning them to death, and returns to his throne in Komar from which he is driven at the conclusion of the fourth book.

DIOMA: A girl of the Red Dragon nation for whose love Athgar risks banishment; later, the mother of Karn.

ELOIGAM: High Priest of Phaolon who weds Karn and Niamh at the end of the fifth book. By an amusing coincidence, he was one of the courtiers who attended Niamh and Karn (then in his *persona* as Chong the Mighty) at the Dance of the Zaiph, which was the beginning of their sequence of adventures.

ERYON: A lord of Komar chained to the oars of the *Xothun* with Karn and Prince Andar.

GOR-YA: Chief of the cave-people at the time Karn and Klygon are captive to them.

GULQUOND: A warrior of Ardha in service to the Temple; it is he who captures Zarqa the Kalood in the second book.

GURJAN TOR: Lord of the Assassins and a mighty power in Ardha. For a brief time, Karn is in his power, and it is in the house of Gurjan Tor that the boy first meets and makes friends with Klygon.

HOGGUR: A minor chief of the Blue Barbarians. He is captain of the galley *Xothun* when Karn and Klygon are rescued from the sea death to which the treachery of Delgan has condemned them. Karn slays him when Prince Andar and the nobles of Komar chained to the oars make their strike for freedom in the fourth book.

HOOM OF THE MANY EYES: One of the Seven
Savants of Sotaspra; a science magician of the Dead
City, and the chief rival of Sarchimus the Wise.

IONA: A girl Amazon of Varda's band who spies on
Karn and her leader.

JANCHAN OF PHAOLON: A prince of the noble
House of the Ptolnim who searches for the lost Niamh
and becomes captive to Sarchimus the Wise; upon the
death of the science magician, he flees from the Scarlet
Pylon with his new friends, Karn and Zarqa the Kalood,
and thereafter shares in their adventures.

KALISTUS: A savant among the Skymen of Calidar,
with Ralidux, a leader of the immortality experiments.
Under the mind-control of Zarqa the Kalood, he assists
the adventures in making their escape from the Flying
City at the end of the third book.

KAORN: A youthful member of Siona's band of forest-
ers, who befriends Chong and Niamh the Fair during
their brief stay in the Secret City in the first book of the
Green Star Saga.

KARN THE HUNTER: A savage boy of the Red
Dragon nation, the son of Athgar and Dioma, who dies
from the venom of the *phuol* at the beginning of the second book, despite the healing arts of Sarchimus the Wise.
The spirit of the hero of the saga enters into his body at
that point, as he had formerly dwelt in the body of
Chong the Mighty, who died at the close of the first
book. It is one of the peculiarities of the saga that nowhere in the five books which comprise it do we learn
the actual name of the central character.

KHIN-NOM: The wise old philosopher and savant of
Phaolon; an officer of Niamh's court who instructs
Chong the Mighty in the customs and language of the
Laonese.

KLYGON THE ASSASSIN: The ugly, loyal, lovable
little man who tutors Karn in the arts of stealth during
his stay in the house of Gurjan Tor and who escapes

with him from Ardha at the beginning of the third book. From that point on throughout the saga, he is Karn's faithful friend and companion during most of his adventures.

LYSIPPUS: A great savant of Calidar, the first to promulgate the dogma that the dwellers of The World Below are savage beasts, not men. From this insidious theory eventuated the madness which overcame the Skymen and perverted their high civilization.

NIAMH THE FAIR: Hereditary Princess of Phaolon who becomes lost among the giant trees with her champion, Chong the Mighty, and comes to love him in both his first and his second incarnation, as Karn the Hunter.

NIMBALIM OF YOTH: The thousand-year-old philosopher whom the adventurers carry to freedom with them when they make their escape from the Flying City of Calidar in the third book. He later joins the court of Prince Parimus of Tharkoon, his fellow sage and scholar.

ONOQUA: Lord chamberlain at the court of Akhmim, Tyrant of Ardha.

OZAD: A baron of Komar; one of the Komarian aristocrats chained to the oars of the *Xothun* with his prince.

PALLICRATES: A prince among the Skymen of Calidar, rival claimant for the throne of Prince Thallius, and leader of the Pallicratian faction which exists to support his ambitions.

PANTHON: A war captain of Phaolon who is in the retinue of Chong the Mighty while he is a resident at the court of Niamh the Fair. It is he who instructs Chong in the use of the Laonese weapons.

PRINCE PARIMUS: Prince-Wizard of Tharkoon; a science magician who lends his powers in aid of Prince Andar's attempt to overthrow the Blue Barbarians then occupying Komar.

PHYRNE: One of Siona's officers; a senior lieutenant of the outlaw band in the Secret City.

PLYCIDUS: A Calidarian patrol leader; it is he who captures Niamh the Fair, Arjala, Prince Janchan, and Zarqa the Kalood at the beginning of the third book.

QUORON OF THE OPAL TOWER: The science magician who enslaves Niamh the Fair to witness his fiendish experiments in the fifth book.

RALIDUX THE MAD: One of the most brilliant of the younger savants among the Black Immortals of Calidar, who conceives of a depraved lust for the goddess Arjala (depraved only in the sense that, according to the dogma of Lysippus, Arjala is a female of a species of beasts rather than a human woman). He is slain by Niamh the Fair at the end of the fourth book.

RKHITH: A giant warrior ant, leader of the legions of the red *kraan* who attack Phaolon.

SARCHIMUS THE WISE: Foremost of the Seven Savants of Sotaspra and Wizard of the Scarlet Pylon. It is Sarchimus who rescues the boy Karn from the *phuol*. However, this action was not prompted by mercy or altruism, but from a desire to possess a live subject on which to test the Elixir of Light.

SHANN OF KAMADHONG: The false identity adopted by Niamh the Fair in the fourth book, during her idyll with Karn on the isle of Narjix, when she pretended to be a boy.

SIONA THE HUNTRESS: Chieftain of the band of forest outlaws who inhabit the Secret City. She fell violently in love with Chong the Mighty after her huntsmen had rescued that warrior and the Princess of Phaolon from the wild.

SLIGON THE BETRAYER: A spiteful outlaw of Siona's band who revealed the secret of Chong and Niamh. In battle he slew the great warrior and was himself slain by Siona.

THALLIUS: Languid, effete young monarch of the Flying City and leader of the Thallian faction.

TRYPHAX: A noble of Komar, condemned to the oar-banks of the *Xothun* together with his prince and his fellow lordlings.

ULTHO: An officer of the Royal Guard of Ardha during the time when Prince Janchan serves among them in disguise, hoping to effect the rescue of Niamh the Fair from the clutches of Akhmin.

UNGGOR: War captain of the Ardhanese Royal Guard who befriends Janchan after the prince helps him defend himself against Gurjan Tor's assassins. He offers Janchan a place in the Guard.

VARDA: A teen-aged girl who leads the band of Amazons who capture Karn in the fifth book. She falls in love with Karn but is spied on by Iona, which leads to her downfall.

XARGO: A former citizen of Kamadhong made captive by the *kraan* and forced to manufacture weapons for the attack against Phaolon. He befriends Zorak during his period of captivity to the insect-creatures.

XIKCHAKA: An injured red *kraan,* or giant ant warrior, with whom Zorak strikes up a comradeship after he is accidentally separated from Niamh the Fair. Of near-human intelligence, the giant insect-creature learns the meaning of friendship from the bowman, the first of his kind to do so since the beginning of the world.

YURGON: Grizzled, kindly lieutenant of Siona's band of forest outlaws who rescues Niamh the Fair from the devil-blossoms and escorts her to the Secret City.

ZARQA THE KALOOD: The last of his kind, the million-year-old Winged Man is the sole surviving member of his extinct race of telepathic humanoids. Their super-scientific achievements include such artifacts as the Flying Cities, the sky-sleds, the living towers of organically grown crystal, the *zoukar* or death-flash, etc. It was their passion for immortality which led to the doom of the Kaloodha; only Zarqa survived, and was a prisoner in the Pylon of Sarchimus the Wise when he first met Karn. Together with Prince Janchan they escaped on the sky-sled, but were soon parted, each to pursue separate adventures until the end of the fifth book.

ZORAK THE BOWMAN: A war officer of Tharkoon who accompanied Prince Parimus in the expedition against the Blue Barbarians who then held the island-city of Komar. When Delgan flies off with Niamh the Fair, it is Zorak who saves her from his clutches.